Hard to Forgive

Georgia Rose

1st Edition Published by Three Shires Publishing

ISBN: 978-1-915665-06-5 (paperback)
ISBN: 978-1-915665-07-2 (hardback)
ISBN: 978-1-915665-05-8 (eBook)

Edited by Mark Barry
www.greenwizardpublishing.blogspot.co.uk

Proofread by Julia Gibbs
juliaproofreader@gmail.com

Cover and map design by Simon Emery
siemery2012@gmail.com

OTHER BOOKS BY GEORGIA ROSE

The Grayson Trilogy

A Single Step (Book 1 of The Grayson Trilogy)

Before the Dawn (Book 2 of The Grayson Trilogy)

Thicker than Water (Book 3 of The Grayson Trilogy)

The Joker (A Grayson Trilogy Short Story)

The Ross Duology

Parallel Lies

Loving Vengeance

A Shade Darker

A Killer Strikes

Shape of Revenge

Table of Contents

A Map of this part of Melton

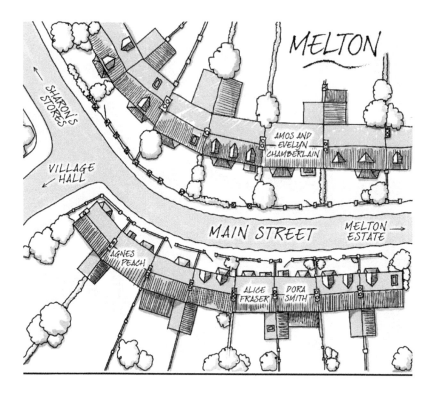

For the original Arran Retreaters – Barb Taub, Darlene Foster and the much-missed Mary Smith. Mary told me afterwards it was a week during which anything seemed possible.
She was right.
This book is testament to that.

Author's Note

Please note that while *Hard to Forgive* is a standalone story it is the third book in the *A Shade Darker* series and I have written these books to be read as a series. I do not rehash what happened in book 1 *A Killer Strikes* or book 2 *Shape of Revenge*, or provide long explanations. From the beginning of this novel, there are spoilers that will affect your enjoyment of both the previous books. Once seen, those things can never be unseen. So, if you haven't read *A Killer Strikes* already you can find it wherever you buy your books. Reading the first in the series before continuing on to *Shape of Revenge* will mean you won't have missed out on meeting those who live and work in The Stables in Melton and the rather wonderful character who takes centre stage in *Shape of Revenge*.

Thank you

Georgia

"The saddest thing about betrayal is that it never comes from your enemies."

Anonymous

Prologue

There is blood on my hand. My fingers wet, tacky. And I stare, shocked at the sight. At the damage I have inflicted.

1: Not the Weather for a Funeral

Now

I usually look forward to a funeral. Prefer them to weddings, in fact. There is less dancing. But that wasn't the case with today's following the horrific murders of the Jackson family. The police have gathered all the evidence they need. They have their man behind bars. And they have released the bodies.

I carry the tray into my front room and place it on the small round table that sits in the bay window. I lift the teapot onto the decorative tile in the centre, add a cup and saucer, a small jug of milk and the side plate on which lies my breakfast. Toast and marmalade. One piece. Cut diagonally.

It is still early, not much past seven, but a lifetime spent as a school secretary has carved routine into my bones and I am incapable of sleeping in. I feel enough of a slouch to be eating breakfast whilst still in my dressing gown. I would never have done that during my working life and that thought makes me pause while I consider whether retirement has made me lax. On balance, probably not. I maintain most standards, and I am certain nothing has slipped so far that the outside world would notice. Everyone there sees what they expect to see. Dora Smith. Spinster of this parish. Ex-school secretary. Pillar of the community. Village treasure.

I do hate that word. Spinster. The equivalent word for a man who has never married is bachelor, which is so much better. Bachelor has a rather dashing rakish edge to it, like they are still desirable, still sexy.

Spinster: the word carries such depressing undertones. Dried-up old husk. Desiccation. But I cannot escape it. I cannot pretend I have spent my life notching up husbands, or even managing one. And as I have lived in Melton my entire adult life, everyone knows exactly what I am.

I sit in my comfy chair, the only seat at this table, place the tray down to one side, then straighten the white linen tablecloth. I pour my tea, add a little milk and reach for a piece of toast. As I eat, I gaze out of the window. The occasional car passes, but other than that, the village is quiet. Daffodil heads bob on the verges on each side of the road. Their sunny yellow muted by the net curtains I view them through. Despite the filter, I can tell it's a bright morning. A fresh spring breeze causes puffs of cloud to scud across the baby-blue sky.

Not the weather for grief.

It will be standing room only, of course, at the church. Probably worse than that, because the entire village has been so consumed by the tragedy. I have heard talk of speakers being set up for those left in the churchyard. I thought I would stay back, be among the outside mourners. I am sure there will be enough family and close friends to fill the church on their own.

Naturally, I knew the Jackson family. Such is the social life in a village. Plus, I enjoyed watching both the girls, Jenny and Judy, grow and flourish over their years at the primary school. But I would not consider myself close to any of them. Also, on this occasion I think I would prefer to be in the churchyard. It might mean standing for the duration, but all that grief trapped inside will be suffocating, pressing in on us like a weighted blanket. At least out in the fresh air, it could dissipate on the bracing March wind.

I have not voiced my thoughts to anyone, because even my friends might consider me cruel, but privately I thought it was just as well the whole family had gone. While I never indulge in gossip, even I have heard disturbing rumours as to what had instigated the attack. Though I found them hard to believe of such a sweet child as Jenny, the oldest daughter. But by all accounts, the murderer had killed the girls first. The thought of John and Jan surviving without them had been almost too much for me to contemplate. No parent should be without their child. I know it happens, but it is against the natural order of things.

As I pour myself another cup of tea, a movement catches my eye and I glance swiftly back out of the window. The front door has opened on the cottage opposite. Amos Chamberlain steps out. His routine is as regimented as mine. I reach for the small pair of binoculars that have permanent residence on my table and lift them to get him in my sights. They are not strictly called for. I have spent my ordered life doing daily eye exercises to avoid the need to wear glasses, but they do add to the drama I like to build into my steady existence.

I see he is using his stick. He fell outside the shop a couple of weeks ago, one wet day in February. I had stayed around to help but it was not appreciated. Nothing broken, but he has limped ever since and is clearly still in need of some support. We don't bounce, or indeed mend, as well, or as quickly, as we once did. That is for sure.

I fancy myself as something of a sleuth. And despite an early setback, I pride myself on being able to sniff out a wrong 'un a mile away. Probably another reason I am single. I never miss a Murder Mystery evening, which is an annual fundraising event in the village, and I know every Agatha Christie novel as if I had written it myself. Miss Marple, my favourite sleuth. If only a crime would present itself, I am sure I would be up to the task of solving it. The recent murders aside, of course. The police have been all over them. Besides, they were decidedly unpleasant, from what I have heard. No, I would prefer something considerably more refined. Someone expiring at the village fete, perhaps, amid the floral bunting and buttered scones, a drop of cyanide having been slipped into their tea. I would impress the hovering crowd by identifying the murder weapon from its almond odour. A spot of light questioning of everyone present would follow. Then I would gather the suspects together and dramatically reveal the culprit who would be carted off by the police. Afterwards we would all sit down to a nice slice of Victoria sandwich and a fresh pot of unadulterated tea. But then, and not for the first time, I have had to consider the distinct possibility I was born at the wrong time.

Therefore, until such an opportunity arises, I must console myself with my second favourite pastime, people watching. I keep my binoculars trained on Amos until he is out of sight. This trip does not particularly interest me. I know he is only off to get his paper from Sharon's Stores. He will be back in less than five minutes. But I make a note in my jotter, anyway. Force of habit.

Once I have cleared away my breakfast things, I prepare for the day ahead. After showering, I open my wardrobe, and reach right to one end to retrieve my only black item of clothing, a dress. Black is such a draining colour and does absolutely nothing for me, so this I save for funerals. As I drag it out, there's a spill of ivory lace from behind it which distracts me for a moment or two. I run the delicate fabric across my fingers before allowing it to fall back into the recesses of the wardrobe.

I dry my hair, taking more care with my neat bob than usual as I am going out. I have never coloured it, despite me thinking it a drab brown earlier in my life. Now I rather like the sophisticated iron grey it has become. I apply makeup. Only a light touch, but it is much needed between the black of my outfit and steel of my hair, otherwise my face might fade away completely. A foundation to even out the complexion. Mascara to highlight eyes that would otherwise disappear. A neutral lipstick. A short while later, I am back sitting at the table in the downstairs window. My favourite seat, from where I watch the world go by.

My stone cottage is in a row that runs along Main Street as it stretches toward the Melton Estate, the old end of the village. A small walled garden, the distance from gate to door being barely three decent strides, fronts each cottage. I have planted roses in my small patch of earth. One trails over the door. Next door Alice has a small table and two chairs. When the weather allows, we often sit out there with a glass of wine to enjoy the evening sun.

There is a similar row of cottages opposite. Similar yet subtly different. The cottages on my side suit singletons, or possibly young couples starting out. Those opposite are a better fit for families. They are consequently wider and set further back from the road with more of a garden out front.

Most of the other cottages are kept in good order, there being a sense of pride about the village. It is quite a sight in the summer months when everything is blooming, and on both sides of the street there is an abundance of hanging baskets. It is the sort of street that ends up on postcards. The exception to all the beauty on display is the gnomes out the front of Agnes Peach's place. Every year she adds more to her collection. The only saving grace is that they are corralled by the wall and largely out of view. I do not mind them, of course, but I know there are some who are glad she is not their direct neighbour.

The funeral is at eleven. I assume Amos will go, but I see several friends and neighbours pass by on the way to the church and there is still no sign of him. It would be odd if he didn't go. He knows the family about as well as I do and with his place in the community – chair of the Parish Council and a driving force behind many village activities, including Shaz's Septuagenarians, the group of volunteers that help at the shop – it is his place to attend. I am on the verge of giving up waiting for him, and am standing, coat on and handbag hanging from the crook of my arm, when his door opens once more and he exits in suitably sombre attire. I count to ten to allow him a head start, then walk out onto the street to follow. If he knows I am there, he gives no indication. But then that's been the case for many a long year.

As we reach the church, satisfactorily distanced, I understand the reason for his late departure. He clearly has the same idea as me. I smile to myself. Great minds think alike. The church is already full, and people stand in small groups in the churchyard. Some even outside the walls, such are the numbers. Conversations are held in low voices all around as I enter the churchyard, the heavy oak gates pinned back for the occasion. The grass has the soggy softness of early spring under foot. Much rain has fallen in recent days and I am thankful I am wearing flat boots and not the shoes I had been considering. Standing some twenty metres away from Amos by the boundary wall, I am near Susannah Bugby, who, among many other things, does the refreshments at the writers' group, and Olivia Croxton, who eats most of them. I add a brief smile to the nod I give both, and as I know they are friends, I ask Susannah where Manda Babcock is. They are rarely seen apart at any gathering. She leans in as though to confide, 'Oh, it's awful. Have yer not heard about the row she had with Sharon? Hasn't been able to leave the house since. I reckon she's got that... what's it called... aggiphobia.'

Petula Cross, as glamorous as ever, wearing a hat with veil, is doing the rounds handing out Order of Service booklets. Susannah reaches to claim our copy. I am hit by a wave of sorrow as I glimpse the family photo on the front and swallow back tears.

'Agoraphobia.' My voice cracks, and I clear my throat before continuing. 'Has she called the doctor?' I knew Susannah would take no notice of the correction, and she ignores my question too, so keen is she to continue with her next piece of news. Her voice is still lowered.

'And, and, guess what? Speaking of Sharon, have you heard what's happened? Eric's only gone and left her. Taken Daisy too. I can't even begin to imagine what's gone on there.' She eyes me. Her beady look ready to pounce on any sign I may know something. I realise she has only shared this with me because I am in a position to add the detail she is missing. But I am well-practised in the art of giving nothing away.

Because this is news I already know, being part of the previously mentioned volunteer group, Shaz's Septuagenarians. A name I deplore, not least because even now I am only sixty-nine. I also know the reason behind Eric and Daisy's departure. Or at least the reason I have been told. That he has another woman. But I don't believe for one moment that is all there is to it. The fact that Daisy has gone too does not quite sit right. Or perhaps I am reading too much into it.

In addition, as I appear to be the volunteer most often called upon, I'm also aware it is not only Manda who is ill. Sharon has been unwell herself and has moaned to me about having been abandoned by her family at such a time. But I mention none of this to Susannah, because it is private and if I did, it would be halfway round the village by the end of the service.

Thankfully, if you can be thankful at such a moment, I can do little more than nod by way of response because a hush falls over the crowd as the hearses arrive. I have never attended a funeral where more than one was needed, and the enormity of the loss hits me again.

As the procession of four coffins makes its way into the church, heads turn and lower. A train of mourners follows. The wider family. I recognise no one, although it is easy to pick out John and Jan's parents. Aged faces drained by grief. I am not sure how they are still standing under the weight of loss. I then spot Laura Brown in the group. It is common knowledge she has returned to her previous married name. She was the closest friend of the Jackson family and yet, after what happened, she must be feeling awful. Still, the wider family clearly attribute no blame in her direction, thank goodness, and I am glad she is included. She has lost weight, her face drawn, and shadows haunt her eyes.

The entourage moves inside and the service starts. There *are* speakers set up and I can hear clearly enough, but some of the emotion of the service is lost listening out here. Not that I mind that. I know I would have cried had I been inside but out in the spring sunshine, as I suspected, I feel a step removed from the intensity, and I am somewhat relieved as a result.

I wonder if Amos is going to the wake at The Red Calf. The pub is not somewhere I often go, what with being single, but occasionally one of my groups meets there, or I will join a friend for a morning coffee and a chat. I like the fact pubs are not all about the alcohol nowadays and make the effort to reach a different audience with decent coffee, excellent cakes and afternoon teas too. I know Mike and Yasmin, the landlords, have put up a marquee in the pub garden to accommodate the expected crowd today. The sound of 'The Lord is My Shepherd' floats across the churchyard and I am relieved to find those of us outside are not expected to sing, although a few join in.

Readings and a poem from the wider family members follow, then beautiful eulogies for each of the family. The vicar speaks movingly and I doubt there is a dry eye among anyone listening.

The sun may be out, but the early March wind cuts like a cheese wire as it whips round the church. I appreciate my full-length wool coat and turn my collar against the icy chill, sinking my chin into the soft folds of my scarf. Despite wearing gloves, I plunge my hands deep into the pockets.

'Freezing, isn't it?' Susannah whispers, leaning close. I merely nod in response, though wonder why she feels it necessary to state something so obvious. She shivers involuntarily. Hardly surprising given she's only wearing a light jacket, the loose scarf at her neck not nearly enough to protect her.

The service ends with a rousing rendition of 'Jerusalem'. Then it is time for the coffins to make a return journey to the hearses. Villagers line the route to see them off. The family, red-eyed and ashen-faced, go off to the crematorium in cars. The church empties, the congregation spreading out across the churchyard like bees from a hive. Once the hearses have left, the atmosphere relaxes marginally and conversations start up

10

once more. Susannah begins with, 'Lovely service,' but as I struggle with the inanity of small talk, I merely agree with her and move away. A few people nod a greeting or smile at me as I pass. Fortuitously, most are already involved in conversations, so I can continue on by without stopping. Of those who speak, the weather is the subject they start with, followed by 'lovely service', something along those lines. Nothing original. If I linger, I suspect discussions would expand into what a tragedy the whole thing is before going down the line of the latest rumour or conspiracy theory. I am not sure if it is because I have spent too much of my life living alone or simply find conversation difficult, quite possibly a combination of the two, but these are all things that do not need saying. To appear polite though, I smile, agree, and add little, so as not to prolong the exchange.

Amos is circulating. He is naturally more gregarious than me and, as always, seems happy to stand and chat. I initially have a job to keep an eye on him in such a large crowd, but it gradually thins as people drift away from the church and towards the pub. I assume Amos will go too, as he likes an excuse to have a pint or two, but he does not. Instead, he eventually separates himself off from those he has been chatting with and, turning down offers to go with them to the Calf, walks towards home. After a suitably discreet period, I follow.

Once home, I quickly change back into something more comfortable. Trousers and a long-sleeved tee-shirt, then add a chunky jumper as it is chilly. I make myself a sandwich and take that and a pot of tea through to the front room where I take up my place at the table for lunch.

The fact Amos has forgone the trip to the pub intrigues me. It is not like him, and it only adds fuel to the fire that has been building in my mind about his recent behaviour. Amos Chamberlain is up to something and I am determined to find out what it is.

2: Moving Day

Then

I did not need a van when I moved into my cottage. My compact car was more than big enough to transport all my belongings. I picked up the keys from the estate agent once completion day arrived and travelled in great excitement to make Melton my new home. I had only seen the cottage once before. So it was with some trepidation that I put the key in the lock and opened the front door. My concern that the cottage might not be as lovely as I had built it up to be in my imagination had caused a few restless nights recently. I had arrived after dark that first night, and only carried in what I needed to see me through until morning. It was not until the next day that I could properly view the property again. I was not disappointed.

The cottage had been vacant for some time, the previous owner having died. I should add they died in hospital rather than in the cottage. I had had quite enough death around me recently to not want it associated with my new home too. Although perfectly placed and sound in structure, it did need a complete update and decoration.

I spent the first night on the floor, which I padded out with towels, and although I covered myself with a blanket, I woke stiff and sore. Years later, I realised how foolish I had been to give away all my parents' furniture. But at the time, everything felt cloaked in grief and I did not want to carry that with me to what I wanted to be a new start.

I was an only child and something of a late miracle, so I was told. It had surprised me to be left enough money by my parents to buy the cottage and I was saddened they had not got to spend it in their old age. Instead, they had died relatively young and within six months of each other. I had never been able to shake the feeling that stress had been the cause. Stress I had brought to their door.

Much as I missed them, I am a practical person, and once I had settled their affairs, I knew I needed to move away and start afresh. Fate decided which area I was to move to, and after all I had been through this part of my life went smoothly. So smoothly, in fact, it confirmed in my mind I was making the right choices.

First, I needed to get a job. I had applied for the role of school secretary at a primary school with no expectation of even getting an interview. But I was contacted within the week, interviewed, and swiftly offered the role, which I gratefully accepted.

Second, I discovered the perfect cottage in the exact location I was looking for up for sale. I made an offer, it was accepted, and the sale went through without a hitch.

I took these two positive outcomes as signs that what I was doing was not ridiculous. It was meant to be.

I spent my first week in Melton scouring second-hand shops in the nearby towns for the minimal amount of furniture I could get away with. In my second week, I began work at the primary school in the next village.

Once I was bringing in a steady wage, I started on the works needed to make my cottage into the home I sorely needed. It took years before I had everything exactly as I wanted it.

I had used the rest of my savings to get the big jobs done first. A new kitchen and bathroom, followed by replacement of the electrics throughout the cottage. Plus, I ensured the property was dry from the foundations up and roof down.

Once those works were complete, I spent evenings, weekends and holidays decorating each room exactly as I wanted it to be. I was happy to do the preparation. Stripping wallpaper, filling where needed, plastering occasionally, then lining and painting. I learned many new skills along the way and enjoyed putting together colour schemes for each room that would blend with the whole.

It wasn't as though I had anyone to share that time with, so I contented myself by pouring my love instead into making my house a home. I kept an eye out for the perfect items of furniture to fill it with. I made curtains and soft furnishings and finally I saved up and had carpets laid throughout, making my cottage the cosy refuge I had always wanted for myself.

Meanwhile, I settled into Melton and became familiar with the surrounding villages. Being the local school secretary meant I quickly became known in the catchment area, at least by the parents of primary school age children. During this time, I also gradually got to know the neighbours where I discovered I wasn't the only recent addition to the village either.

Buying this cottage in Melton might not have been part of my original plan. But things change and naturally one must adapt.

3: Amos Goes Visiting

Now

I am wondering why Amos did not go to the wake, as it appears he has nothing better to do with his day when he emerges from his house once more. He has also changed and now wears the tan corduroys I like, and his thickly quilted jacket that does nothing for the figure. His paper is clamped under his arm. The sky has darkened, and rain is forecast. I note he has added a tweed cap which also does him the favour of covering his receding hairline. He could do with a haircut. I noticed earlier it was tatty around his ears and too long at the back. He never looked this untidy while Evelyn was around. My stomach twists at the thought of her. I suppose that is the thing with long marriages. If you are the one left behind, it is difficult to keep on top of all the things you used to get reminded to do. It is one bonus to remaining single. You never rely on anyone else.

Checking back in my jotter to last Tuesday, I note he went out at the same time then too. I look up again. He is walking toward the shop. I consider following him, but it would be too obvious in a virtually deserted village street. On the way to and from the church, it was expected. Now, he will spot me in an instant, and if he is up to something, which I suspect he is, he will alter his behaviour, and I do not want that.

Time passes. I could do with a visit to the lavatory, but dare not leave my post for fear I will miss Amos's return and will not have a proper record of how long he was out for. I try to distract myself, reaching for a photo album from the bookshelves behind me. It is one of my early ones. Photo scraps. Not much

16

more than that. But precious, nonetheless. Ancient and yellowing scallop-edged photos of parents. Deckchairs. Seaside donkeys. Vehicles from another age, with seats that scalded bare legs in summer. A baby swaddled tight. Groups of friends. Hugging. Laughing. Picnics on the sand. The family dog. All black and white. All another lifetime. Tears well up, and I close the album with a sigh for what could have been.

I stare back out through the nets. Curtain-twitcher. That is another description that could be levelled in my direction. A rather derogatory term, I think. Besides, the curtains never do twitch. Not if you are a professional.

The waiting is most frustrating, but I sit, eventually cross-legged, my foot jigging, until I see him walk back up the road. Nothing has changed in his appearance, and he still has his paper. But he has been gone two hours. Where could he have been for two hours in Melton? None of the groups meet at this time. It occurs to me he could have simply gone to the wake. But why would he have eschewed going with his friends, only to change his clothes and go there an hour later? That made no sense at all.

He would not have gone for a walk for this length of time either. You could walk every pathway in Melton and it would not take an hour, let alone two. And he was not kitted out for hiking. Footwear-wise, I mean. I have been watching Amos for a lifetime, and exercise has never been part of his daily activity, so hiking across the countryside would be a stretch. Plus, of course, he is still walking with a stick following his fall, therefore it is hardly the time to increase his step count.

I note the time, then pop to the lavatory before updating my records. When I check back on my notes, this is in fact the third Tuesday in a row, he has gone out at the same time for two hours. And it is not the only new pattern forming recently. He was once a regular at the Wednesday Coffee Morning (10 'til noon) but had missed the last four weeks. Even though I had seen him leave his house at the same time as if he was going to attend it, he never arrived at the village hall. No one there had known where he was, either. Something similar was happening Friday afternoons too. I sit back in my chair and think. Before next Tuesday, I have to come up with a plan as to how I can find out where he is going.

I get up and stretch, before wandering through to the kitchen to see what I have got in for dinner. It is unlikely Amos will move far from home now. None of our groups meet this evening, and the only time he goes out otherwise is to the pub. Which usually coincides with an event, such as a darts match or a pool tournament. He is not one for going drinking just because. I have to say one thing for Evelyn, she got him into good habits. And he has never put a foot out of place. In fact, neither of them ever have. Impeccably behaved lives. That is what they have lived. And I should know, I've been watching them for long enough.

The thing is, while *I* know he has not led a blameless life, everyone around here thinks he is some sort of saint. He is so damned worthy and I would have liked to have caught him out, if only once, doing something he should not. Purely to show the village he is not as perfect as everyone believes him to be. I glance back at my records and wonder if an opportunity may be about to present itself.

One can always hope.

4: The Big Day

Then

Waking with a buzz of excitement thrumming through my veins, I threw back the covers and leapt out of bed to rush to the window and check on the weather. Settled for a few days now, there was no suggestion it wouldn't hold for one more. The perfect summer's day. I wrapped my dressing gown around myself as I approached my wardrobe. My dress had been hanging there since Mum pressed it yesterday. I caught hold of the edges of the veil, stretched my arms to spread the lace wide, then let it fall back in ivory folds, lace on satin. I rushed from the room, my steps light like a dancer as I ran downstairs and into the kitchen.

'I am getting married today,' I exclaimed to a room populated only by people who knew that already. My parents. Mum, wraparound apron on as always, rose from the table to cut a couple of slices from the loaf, then placed them under the grill. Dad lowered his newspaper to peer at me over the top of his glasses.

'Ahh, yes, I knew I had something on today.' His paper lifted once more.

Ignoring Dad's dry comment, I turned to Mum. 'Nothing for me, thanks. I cannot eat a thing.' She put her hands on my shoulders and gently pressed me into a chair.

'You must have something in your stomach, love, or you'll be passing out later.' She knew me well. I sighed but stayed still and ate the buttered toast and drank the tea, despite my stomach churning with nerves, threatening to reject them at any moment.

The morning disappeared in a whirl of getting ready. It was only going to be a small affair. A handful of family from our side and a few close friends would be at the church and go back to The Snipe and Partridge for the buffet they had laid on after. But, here in the village of Crowthorne, we were well known, my parents active participants in the church. Many more would turn out to see their only child get married. To wish us well. It was what I loved about life there.

My best friend and only bridesmaid, Beth, arrived to help me get ready, and we rushed giggling up the stairs, neither quite believing this day had finally arrived. We had been friends since primary school, maintaining a friendship that had survived right through our recent stint at secretarial college. Our paths were now diverging. While Beth was heading to London in a couple of days to take up a prestigious personal assistant position for the manager of an hotel, I was settling down to married life. One, I hoped, that would be blessed with children. Having a family was the only thing I had ever wanted.

Beth and I had spent a lot of time in my bedroom. Dressing up as children, doing each other's hair and makeup as we grew up, laughing over boys, sharing secrets. Today felt different, poignant somehow. The end of an era, or for us, a lifetime. Beth told me she had packed her cases for her trip to London. Mine were similarly ready in the corner of my bedroom for the move into our first home together as man and wife. Beth and I made the most of our final few hours together, pushing down the tears that threatened to rise. Mum was no better, her eyes red-rimmed when we met in the garden mid-morning to cut flowers for the bouquets.

My mind drifted to thoughts of my fiancé. Beth and I pondered how well he was feeling. I had last seen him two days ago, and he had been due to have his stag do that evening. A few friends. A trip to the pub. That was all. I hoped he had not overdone it. I imagined him getting ready in the flat we had rented together in town rather than the village, as it was handier for his job, and, fresh out of college, I was more likely to find work there too.

At eleven-thirty, we were all ready. Dad popped the cork on a bottle of fizz and called us downstairs. He was waiting in the sitting room as I made my entrance and he swelled with pride. My dress was simple and elegant, the points of my shoes peeking out from below the hem. Mum made both our dresses from a pattern we girls chose together. Beth's was cut in the same style but was three-quarter length and in a cornflower blue that highlighted her eyes beautifully. Mum wore a new navy dress and jacket, her pillbox hat fixed securely in place.

I had to admit we had come together well, and I could not stop smiling as Dad passed round the glasses he swore were necessary to take the edge off our nerves. He was probably right; he usually was. Mine fluttered in my stomach like a startled kaleidoscope of butterflies.

I finished my glass and checked the clock on the mantelpiece. It was time to go, and I was anxious not to be late. Whatever a bride's prerogative might be.

With a keen eye on the budget, I had refused my father's offer to hire a fancy car and thought it would be nicer to go on foot. As I walked out of my family home for the last time as a single woman, I was delighted to see my dad hold out his arm. I linked mine through his, thankful for his support, both now and throughout my life.

Mum and Beth followed, and we smiled and waved at neighbours who cheered us from windows and gardens, pavements and verges, as we headed towards the church.

I was beaming as we passed through the lychgate and took the path through the churchyard. The sun was out, the faintest breeze enough to freshen the air and keep us cool. As we approached the doors, the vicar was there, come to greet us. Which I was not expecting, but was a lovely reassuring touch.

I had known him all my life, a friend of the family. He held out his hands to mine, and I switched my bouquet into the hand linked through my dad's arm and reached out my free one, which he wrapped in his own. I smiled. I thought he was about to impart some wisdom. About to say the words he had said to countless brides before me.

'Well,' he said, 'here we all are then. You look beautiful.' I blushed at the compliment. There was an infinitesimal change. His smile faltered as he pinned it in place but he failed to keep his gaze from sliding away from mine. He continued, 'All we need now is the groom.'

My stomach lurched at what could only be a mistake. I needed to pass him, to plunge on into the church, to see his absence for myself. Dad held me back. Told me to keep calm.

'Have you heard anything from him at all?' Dad asked. The vicar shook his head. 'Nothing from his best man?' Another shake.

'We will wait,' I said, with every confidence. 'He will have been held up. He will be here in a minute.' The vicar merely inclined his head in acknowledgement, squeezed my hand and let it go. I turned to look at Mum, at Beth, refusing to show anything other than total faith. 'He will be here in a minute,' I repeated under my breath as I turned back, the words for me as much as anyone else.

The door to the church was closed, but we could hear a murmur from behind it. Family. Friends. Restless.

I wasn't wearing a watch, so had a surreptitious glance at Dad's. He noticed.

'That'll not get him here any quicker.' He patted my hand. I glanced behind again. A small group had gathered at the churchyard gate, waiting for us to emerge after the service. There were a couple of craning necks. A nudge here and there. Curiosity over our lack of progress. I took a step closer to the door, moved Dad along with me, to get out of view.

The vicar and my parents were talking about the weather. Warmer here in the porch. No air flow. Mum took out the fan that was a permanent accompaniment in those days. She flicked it open with a practised wrist. Beth leaned in to fiddle with the folds of my veil and I tried not to let it irritate me. I closed my eyes.

'Dora,' the vicar said, his voice gentle. They opened again.

'He must have had an accident.' I took a good hard look at Dad's watch. Ten minutes late. Actually, half an hour as he was going to be here by twenty to. He had promised. "See you in church," his last words to me. The words of a man who was going to be there.

'Whatever the reason for his non-appearance. I think we need to decide what we do now.' I could see he did not believe me about the accident.

My Uncle Jimmy chose that moment to open the door to the church and stick his head out. His face brightened at the sight of us.

'Hello, angel, am I pleased to see you,' he said. 'I thought both of you was gonna be a no show.' My determination wavered at his words. He slipped through the door, closed it behind him. My dad, Jimmy's brother, took charge.

'Jimmy, can you go back in and tell everyone there will be no wedding today and they should make their way over to the pub? You can take it from there.' There was no discussion over what might have caused my fiancé to not turn up and it annoyed me. It appeared they had all jumped to the conclusion he had jilted me. Like there could be no other explanation. Like they had no faith in him. They had not shown this before. Yes, they had been concerned about the age gap. I was nineteen, he was twenty-eight. Yes, they thought it odd he had no family to come to the service, but that was hardly his fault. Despite these minor concerns, they had appeared supportive of my choice, right up until this moment.

'Dad,' I protested. 'They might as well go home.'

'There's no point in all the food and drink going to waste. It's bought and paid for.' There was a harsh edge to his words, and I sensed his growing anger. Jimmy turned to go, then glanced back at me.

'You look knockout, angel. He's a fool.'

'Thank you.' I caught the vicar's eye; he looked at me kindly.

'I'm sorry, Dora. This is a horrible thing to have happened. He seemed...' He tailed off. *Exactly*, I thought, finishing the vicar's words in my head. *He seemed lovely. That is because he is lovely. There is no way he would have jilted me. Absolutely no way.* Something must have happened, and I needed to find out what.

'Come on,' I said, turning around to face Mum and Beth, 'I do not want to still be here when that lot comes out,' and I jerked my head toward the church door. Dad held out his arm again, and I latched on to it as though he was the only thing keeping me up. And in that moment, I desperately wished we had a car ready and waiting to whisk us home.

Either way, we would still have had to run the gauntlet of the crowd at the gate. It fell silent as we approached. I kept my eyes downcast. I couldn't bear to see the sympathetically tilted heads, the looks of pity. Shame burned my cheeks because they would all think I had been left at the altar, too. I could not wait to get back and find out what had happened, to reassure myself that, if there had been an accident, no one had been badly hurt.

I glanced over at the pub, its door decorated with ribbons in honour of our celebrations.

'They're all bastards, if you ask me,' someone shouted. Something of a generalisation, but solidarity nonetheless with my perceived predicament. A murmur of approval followed.

Never had the journey back from the church lasted as long. Tears bit, and pain grew in my throat at the threat of them, but I blinked them away and swallowed, not giving in right now. Not in front of everyone. As we walked, I planned out my course of action. We did not have a telephone at the house, still relying on the kiosk down the road, but it would not have helped even if we did because we did not have one at the flat either. I was going to have to go there in person instead. Although it was unlikely he was there, otherwise why was he not here? While my thoughts raced ahead, I fully expected to see him on the side of the road on the way, broken down and frustrated.

There were still plenty of villagers out and about to see my return. Their eyes burned into me. No one said anything, there was no need. News travelled fast in a village. Bad news fastest of all.

I was relieved when we were back at our door. I walked straight into the front room, then turned to face the others.

Mum had her arms wide, and I knew she wanted to give me a hug, but if she was nice now, I would cry and I needed to keep going, so I brought my hands up to fend her off. 'Not now, Mum, I can't bear it. I have to find him. He must have broken down or had an accident.' Her tears were not far away, but she nodded briskly, although I did not feel much conviction flowing from her.

'Dad? Can you take me to the flat please?'

'Damn right I can.' He never cursed, so I knew he was furious. I could see it in the set of his jaw, and I did not much like having to hunt my fiancé down with him around as I dreaded to think what he would do when we found him. But I had no other choice. Mum could not drive, and I had not taken my test yet.

'I will go and change. Beth, can you help me?' She followed me upstairs with none of the joy we had had earlier.

'What do you think has happened?' she asked tentatively as she helped me out of my dress.

'Like I have said, I can only assume an accident. Or he has broken down. What else could it be?' She remained quiet. 'I need to get into town, Beth. He might need me. He might be in the hospital.'

There was a long pause, before she said. 'Don't you think Mick would have managed to get a message to us if that were the case?' She came round to face me.

'Not if they had an accident on the way. They will be together after all. They could both be hurt.' Mick Archer was the best man and whatever she was insinuating, I was not having it.

26

I hung my dress up, the veil too, as I was sure I was going to be putting it on again soon. Although even as I thought about it, I decided we would have to go to a registry office instead. I could not put my parents through the expense again. Thoughts like this tumbled around my brain and I took a deep breath and an active decision to stop thinking down those lines. All I needed to do right now was drive to town with Dad and find out what had happened.

Beth had changed out of her dress too and I made her hang it up alongside mine, in readiness. I dressed in light trousers and a casual shirt, and we went back downstairs.

'Do you want me to come with you?' she asked. I placed my hand on her arm.

'No thanks, but would you stay with Mum until we get back?'

'Of course.' When we walked into the kitchen, Mum was deliberating whether to put her apron on over her wedding outfit. Beth turned to her with a smile on her face and took the apron from her hand. 'I'll get the kettle on while you get changed if you like.' They had always got on, and I knew she would be good company for Mum while we were gone.

Dad was out of his suit too and clutched the car keys in his hand.

'Shall we go?' I said, and I led the way out of the front door, appearing braver than I was feeling. The only thought keeping me going was my fear of finding my fiancé badly injured in a hospital and of him being alone and needing me to be with him.

5: An Absence and an Arrival

Now

There is a coffee morning in Melton every Wednesday. It has been running for more years than I care to remember. When I was working, I often used to bake some biscuits or a cake and drop these off at the hall before driving to school. Looking back, I am not sure why I did that when I could not attend, other than it made me feel like I was still supporting the village. And appearing to be a good person, I suppose. Anyway, since I retired, I usually go along, although I prefer to busy myself making tea and coffee than actually partaking in any of the chat.

Many of the oldies attend along with some of the young mums and their babies and toddlers. We have created a play area with trikes and suchlike at one end of the hall, where the youngsters can use up some energy.

Amos left his cottage earlier, so I am surprised when I get to the village hall and there is no sign of him. Susannah Bugby is behind the counter I slide my lemon cake onto.

'That looks delicious, thank you. I'll cut it up,' and she drags the plate closer and starts slicing into it with a knife only one size smaller than a machete.

'You are welcome. No sign of Amos again then?' I say, as casually as I can manage.

'No, he did say that he wouldn't be coming for a few weeks, though.'

'Oh, I hadn't heard that. Got a better offer, has he?' I wrestle the coffee machine out of the cupboard.

She laughs. 'Better than coffee and cake at the village hall? What could match that?'

What indeed? I think.

The door bursts open with the force only an exuberant toddler can bring to the action, and this particular one charges down to the play area. I see his exhausted mother enter behind, pushing a baby in a pram, and rush to get the coffee machine going. Someone looks like they need a shot of caffeine.

While I busy myself with getting organised, more people arrive, and the atmosphere is alive with chat and laughter. There is a friendly community in this village and regular events like this mix old and young, and keep everyone in touch. Sally Button must be off work as I can see her pushing the pram up and down the hall in an attempt to give the young mum a break. Her kindness makes me smile. She has had a rotten start to the year herself but is back doing what she can to help others.

A short while later, she joins me in the kitchen and says, 'Are you still on for the Murder Mystery?'

'Yes, of course. I hope you are? How will the murder ever be solved without the top crime-fighting duo on the case?' We both laugh, but then she brings up the point we haven't discussed. The lack of numbers for our table. And that stops the laughter. Usually, John and Jan Jackson would be with us. Maisie Brooks too, but she was away caring for her parents in Spain and as her cottage opposite The Stables is currently advertised for rent, it didn't look like she was coming home anytime soon. I had already considered the issue. 'I thought we could ask Laura, Harry and Pip from The Stables and perhaps Olivia and Kyle too. That would give us seven if they could all come.' I had thought it might be nice for Laura and those who worked with her to come to a village event. I had not seen them out and about at all and I thought back to how thin Laura looked at the funeral yesterday. Olivia and Kyle Croxton were a nice young couple who lived in a cottage opposite The Stables, adjacent to the one owned by Maisie Brooks. I had thought that group would already know each other too, which would make for a more comfortable evening.

'Sounds perfect. Shall I ask them, or will you?'

'I'm in the shop Friday, so I'm bound to see some of them, otherwise I will catch them over the weekend.' A child howls from the play area and, distracted, Sally moves towards the door.

'Great, let me know if you need me to do anything.'

'Will do,' and I turn back to carry on with the washing up. Once I am up to date with that, I am aware there is a danger I am going to run out of useful jobs to do and will have to talk to someone. I dry my hands, put on my coat and collect my now empty plate before I check in with Susannah.

'Everything okay if I head off now? Coffee is made, the teapot is full and there are plenty of biscuits for any latecomers.'

'Of course. But you've been busy and haven't even had a coffee yourself? Why don't you get one and come over to the table to join us?'

'Thanks, but I'm expecting a delivery and need to get back.'

'Okay then. You don't want to be missing that.' I give Sally, who is marshalling the activity in the play area, a quick wave before I leave. I walk out into a rain shower I was not expecting. Fortunately, the village hall is not far from home, and I duck my head down, as though I think it will help, and hurry.

As I round the corner into Main Street, I stop abruptly because I spot Amos. He is just leaving the home of Agnes Peach but does not see me as he walks to her gate and lets

30

himself out onto the pavement, closing it carefully behind him. I stand and watch as he continues up the road, then crosses over to his own property and lets himself in. That explains why he never got to the coffee morning, but it does not shed light on why he would be spending time with the mostly housebound Agnes Peach. She is rarely seen out nowadays and when she is, it is with the aid of a walking frame or her niece, who can sometimes come and lend a hand. Amos has always been sniffy about Agnes's gnomes too, an attitude I am sure was cultivated by Evelyn. And I don't think he and Agnes had ever been particularly friendly but perhaps with Evelyn gone, Amos is not so fussy about the company he keeps.

Once Amos is safely behind his own front door, I continue my walk home pondering the relationship he might have with Agnes. Evelyn has been gone five years now. It comes as a shock to realise how swiftly that time has passed. But as I think it, something utterly distasteful springs to mind. Maybe... and I can barely believe I am even thinking this, but maybe he still has needs that want satisfying. It is not something I had considered before, and I don't want to now, but if something is going on between him and Agnes, is Agnes in full enough control of her faculties to consent to it? I am not so sure. The whole idea is such a deeply unpleasant one though, it makes me queasy, so I determine that now it has been given some consideration, I will attempt to dispel it from my mind as nonsense.

The next day is Thursday and I have a few extra bits and pieces to do in the morning because Ned is coming round in the afternoon. He is the local handyman, although he probably prefers to be called a builder. That is what it says on his van:

General Builder. No job too small. Specialities – extensions and loft conversions. Although I have never known him to be involved with either. Maybe once upon a time, in his prime, but now he is known as the odd-job man, and consequently is in high demand.

He checks in with me every week or two, comes round if I have any things for him to do. Between visits I keep a pad on the side and every time I notice a loose door handle, a squeaking hinge, a dripping tap, I make a note. Then Ned arrives to put it all right again. He is useful and I look forward to his visits. He lives further afield, but his client base has developed over the years around the village of Melton, and that and the surrounding area keeps him in full-time work.

He was only here last week, but one hinge broke on the door to the larder and I am struggling to open and close it, so he said he would pop in. He arrives at lunchtime, as expected.

'Have you had time for something to eat this week?' I ask as I wave him in through the front door. I know he is always rushing from one job to the next, and often does not find the time for food. He is in his overalls, his tool bag carried in front so as not to mark the walls.

'No, no, but don't you worry, love, I'll be fine.' He puts his tools down on the sitting room carpet. 'Now, it's just the hinge, is it?'

'Absolutely not,' I admonish him. 'You are not starting until you have had a bowl of soup.' I point through to the kitchen to where there are two places set at the table.

A broad grin lights up his face. 'Dora, you're an angel.'

'It is the least I can do. Besides, you are the one doing me the favour. At least it is one meal I do not have to eat alone.' I ladle soup into bowls and carry them to the table. A basket of crusty bread is between us and I tell him to help himself.

'How has your week been?' I ask, and between spoonfuls he tells me what he has been up to since he was last here. It is strange but while I find it difficult to strike up a conversation with most people, I never have any problem talking to him.

Later, I shift my weight, throw my pale leg over his tanned one and curl into his side as we lie in bed together. My larder door is fully attached, and I have had a decent orgasm. It has been a good day.

The carnal side of our relationship started a few years ago.

I daresay it would shock some. Maybe they would think we are too old. But exactly when should you stop having sex? Besides, I have missed out on plenty throughout my life, and see no reason I should not make up for it now.

Privately, I call him my boyfriend and delight in knowing I am someone's girlfriend. If those descriptions are not too weird at our ages. He is some ten years younger than I am, which means technically he could also be my toy boy but that is a step too far. And I have never mentioned it to Ned, as I do not think he even knows how old I am. I have often been told I look young for my age. Certainly, without the stresses and strains maintaining a marriage and family can put on a woman, I am confident in the state of my body. Other than the fact that for the whole of my life it has been decidedly underused for any matters of a sexual nature.

Over the years, I have realised that finding love in a village, when you are not a particularly sociable creature, is not easy. You only have to take a look round at the possible candidates to realise there is not one among them that actually inspires you.

Then, by the time online dating became possible I thought I was past it and, if I were being honest, felt the whole thing to be a bit sordid. Of course, there is also the trust issue. It was always going to be difficult for me to put my trust in someone again, and the chances of me doing so with a man I met on the internet were zero. This situation suits me. Although it is a shame our relationship has to be kept secret.

As a rule, I do not agree with adultery, but the position I am in with Ned has taught me I should not be so swift to judge. Sometimes there are mitigating factors why it is necessary.

I had been a user of Ned's handyman skills for a couple of years before he confided in me. We had always chatted while he was working, anyway. Him being one of few people I enjoy talking to because he somehow makes me feel comfortable. I would make him tea or coffee; provide biscuits and we would have a catch-up while he had a break. Sometimes, if the job took longer, I would offer him lunch. It seemed rude to be making some for myself and not him. He would join me at the kitchen table and we would carry on talking and found we got on. I knew he had a wife and grown-up children and one day he announced they had another grandchild on the way. It was as he told me this his voice had broken. I had automatically reached out and placed my hand on his for comfort.

'What is it? What's wrong?'

'I'm sorry. I rarely get upset. It must be the thought of the grandchild. It's making me soft.'

'I don't think you are being soft. Is everything okay?' He had shaken his head, chewed his lip as though deciding how, or if, to continue.

'There's something I haven't told you, Dora. It's one of those things where it's difficult to judge when it's the right time to share something with someone. But I think we know each other well enough for me to confide in you. If you want me to, of course?'

Intrigued, of course I said yes, and then it all came out. Ned's wife was suffering from early onset dementia. After being cared for at home for years, she could no longer recognise him or their children and now lived in a specialist care home. He told me she would have no understanding of what a new grandchild would mean for the family, or the joy it would bring. It was this Ned was understandably finding hard to bear.

My heart had gone out to him. Completely and utterly. It was a terrible position to be in and now I knew about his situation, I could clearly see how sad and lonely he was. Why he was happy to chat away as he worked. Why he enjoyed staying for a bite to eat. He had got up from the table to continue with his work then and as I stood too, I had gone to hug him, not able to remember the last time I had hugged anyone. We had held each other for comfort and as he had pulled away, I had kissed him. A peck on the cheek, not much more, and I was not sure why I did it but it stopped him in his tracks. He tentatively touched his lips to mine, and I kissed him back. And so, our affair began. He was lonely, and someone I already trusted, which was a first after many years. But naturally, out of respect for his wife, we had kept it behind closed doors. Despite that I looked forward to his visits as eagerly as a teenager. I embarrassed myself actually counting down the days until I saw him again and he had brought a light into my life that had been missing for a long time. I think he felt the same as me because more than once he had hinted at us having a future and although that was an impossibility right now, it still made me feel loved and reassured. In the meantime, he came round when he could, when it would not raise any suspicion, and the arrangement suited us both just fine.

Recently I have realised two things. This is the longest relationship I have ever had with a man, which is not exactly what I intended for my life. And, I have fallen in love. I had tasted love before, but once lost, found it was not so easy to come by a second time and had unexpectedly ended up living my life alone. Until now.

Falling in love at this age is different. Death is so close you can almost reach out and touch it. There is no holding back, no time for games or recriminations on the nature of our relationship. It is what it is, most likely the last love affair of our lives and as such is glorious, unexpected and feels as though gold rains down upon us as we cherish and nurture what we have. We both accept that and make the most of the limited time we get to spend together.

Any loneliness I feel is certainly not caused by the absence of a man in my day-to-day existence.

After Ned has left, I sit watching out of the front window. I have no desire to be spotted, therefore I keep my curtains open, but lights off, in case there is any movement over the road. My mind is unsettled, but I am not sure why. When I think through everything that has happened recently, I consider the fact it may be down to my thoughts on the possible relationship between Amos and Agnes. Maybe the reminder of Evelyn's death? That never helps my spirits. I look around my sitting room as a distraction and wonder if I should get Ned to redecorate to freshen it up, but I cannot even decide on that. I suppose I could do it myself. It would not be the first time.

6: The Aftermath

Then

I ignored the curious glances that came our way as we walked out to the car. There wouldn't usually be this many people around. No doubt they were loitering in the hope of hearing or seeing something of the drama going on in our lives. I was thankful when we had left the village and were away from the stares.

We drove in silence. Dad, grim determination on his face as he gripped the steering wheel. Me, keeping an anxious eye out for a broken-down car, or any sign of an accident. But there was nothing.

As we approached the outskirts of town, Dad said, 'We'll go to the flat first, okay?'

'Yes.' Although I was not sure what we would do afterwards. Check at the hospital? Try to find the pub he had had his stag night in? *One step at a time*, I told myself.

We pulled up to the curb outside the Victorian terrace we were going to call home. The small property was divided into two flats. Ours was upstairs and tiny, but it was enough to give us a start. We had only picked up the keys a week ago. One for the outside door that led into a lobby and the stairs which took us up to our front door. I had not even moved my things in yet. We were going to go away for a couple of nights to a hotel on the coast immediately after the wedding, then come back and move in properly together. Our first home.

'Do you want me to come with you?' Dad asked, placing his hand on mine.

'No. I think I need to do this on my own.' He nodded, withdrew his hand, and I reached for the handle to get out.

The net curtain twitched in the window of the downstairs flat. I knew our landlady lived there, but I had not met her yet. I took out my keys and let myself in, then trotted up the stairs that rose through the musty space, painted a peculiar mottled green. It was as if splotchy mould had erupted on the walls and seeped through the paint like invading armies of bacteria. On our initial viewing, I had immediately decided I was going to ask if I could paint this grim communal space. Make it my first task.

I reached our front door, and as I inserted my key, I took a deep breath. I wasn't sure what I was expecting to find on the other side, but I had not considered it would be nothing. Yet I opened the door to the same empty space it had been when we viewed it. Since then, my fiancé had told me he had moved a few of his things in. A bed had been delivered, supposedly. At least that's what he had led me to believe. He was also meant to have stayed here last night, to get ready for our wedding today. Yet there was nothing to show for his presence. No bed. No clothes. No sign anyone had been here.

For the first time, my faith in him faltered. I did not understand what was going on. Where was he? Where were his things? Maybe he had had a change of heart and decided he wanted us to move in together after our wedding? Let it be a new start for us both. But then there had not been a wedding, so where did that leave us now?

I heard shuffled footsteps behind me, someone climbing the stairs, slowly. Breath wheezing. An elderly woman pushed the door open, one arm on the doorframe supporting her. She wore a wraparound apron, floral, a palette of orange and brown. A cigarette protruded from wizened lips. Her skinny forearms were bare, sleeves rolled back. Her skin pallid and dry, wrinkled at the elbow.

My landlady had not been around when I had viewed the place and was not coming across as the sympathetic sort.

''e said you'd be round,' she said as smoke curled upward, causing her to squint. She thrust a bony hand into her camouflaged front pocket and withdrew an envelope. 'Got this to give yer.'

I took a couple of steps closer, reached out my hand to take it. 'When did he give you this?'

'Yesterday. Right bloody nuisance, too. Messing me about. An' I'll 'ave yer keys off yer an' all.' My fingers close tight around them.

'No. I am moving in.'

'Not according to 'im yer not. An' he's the one payin' the rent. Tho' I told 'im 'e's lost 'is deposit.' She thrust a threatening finger in my direction. 'Don't yer be thinkin' yer'll be gettin' that back.' She had a point about the rent. I did not have a job yet, and realistically, I was unlikely to afford a place on my own even when I had one, at least initially. My hand hovered over hers, let the keys drop into her palm. I expected her to leave, but she remained. Nodded at the envelope in my hand.

'You gonna open it?' I looked down. The once white envelope was grubby, my name carelessly scrawled on the front.

'Could you give me some privacy?' She tutted, like I had ruined her entertainment, but turned to make her way back down the stairs.

'Close the door when yer leave,' she called back, then after another moment, 'and don't be long. I'm doin' this outta the goodness in me 'eart, I don't want yer takin' advantage.'

I walked across the room and leaned against the windowsill for support, all the while not taking my eyes from the envelope. I was more confused than ever and while I knew the answers to my many questions lay inside, I hesitated to open it. Dreading what I would find when I did.

As I put the moment off, I wondered how long my landlady would give me before she was back up the stairs. But there was not only her to think about. I couldn't keep Dad waiting forever and while I considered taking the letter home and dealing with it there, I knew I needed to know what was going on. I ripped it open. There was a single sheet inside. A few lines.

Dora

You'll know by now we are no longer getting married. I'm sorry I couldn't tell you in person, but you know I can't bear to see you upset. I'm afraid to tell you I've met someone else. It happened very recently and was love at first sight. There was no way I could go through with a wedding to someone I didn't love as deeply.

I hope you can forgive me.

He had signed it with his full name, like it was a business letter.

Stunned. My head swam, and I gasped, leaning one hand against the wall in support as I took a couple of deep breaths. I reread

40

the note. He had met someone else? Since his last words to me, not two days ago, that he would see me in church, he had met someone else? I never expected this. Not for one teeny tiny moment. If I was being honest with myself, the worst I had imagined was he had got cold feet. I had almost been expecting that. I had thought maybe I would be able to talk him around, get things back on track. But this? This was... this was... outrageous. As I thought that word, anger flared deep inside like the molten core of a volcano. How dare he? How dare he treat me like this? Putting aside the whole meeting someone and falling in love bit, because, small point, we were also meant to be in love. He had certainly told me he loved me often enough. Or had it all been lies? So, putting aside the whole meeting someone and falling in love bit, how could he let me turn up to the church knowing I was going to be made a fool of? How could he show me such little respect? How was that loving me?

I'm sorry I couldn't tell you in person, but you know I can't bear to see you upset.

No. Confrontation. That is what he couldn't bear. I had expected my future husband to be many things. A coward was not one of them.

7: Another Piece of the Jigsaw

Now

Sharon booked me to come and assist in the shop on Friday afternoon. It irks me she still takes advantage of Shaz's Septuagenarians. Particularly, mostly me as I appear to be the only still active volunteer in the group. I constantly want to say no to her requests. But there is always some valid reason she needs help. On this occasion, I am one of only a few who are aware Sharon is not well, and she told me she has a doctor's appointment, so I can hardly tell her where to stick it. At least not out loud. It is not what "Village Treasures" do.

The volunteer group was great at first. The shop had been closed for a few years, and it delighted everyone when Sharon, one of our own, wanted to buy the property and open it up again. She got it for a good price and I know she received some grants to get set up, but she still needed support. That is where we stepped in. It was actually Amos, and Evelyn, of course, who came up with the idea of the volunteer group, and I was happy to join and help when I could, bearing in mind I was still working.

However, Sharon is now taking the piss. Pardon my language. The shop is doing well and she could easily pay for a few hours' help. But she does not, preferring to exploit the volunteer group, and mostly me, instead. It occurs to me Shaz's Septuagenarians should have another meeting soon to see how often anyone else is helping. A change is needed and I know a few hours of paid work would be a helpful top-up to my pension.

I arrive shortly before two o'clock. I know Sharon needs to be away soon after, and with the shop quiet, we do a quick handover. She looks terribly pale and her hand shakes as she runs through her list of things to tell me. None of which are important.

'I hear Ned was round at yours yesterday.' I am surprised by this comment as she rarely brings up any subject with me that is not about her. Unless she is digging for information, of course, and potential gossip. Ah, yes. That must be it.

'Yes, a hinge had broken on the larder door and he came by to fix it.' She smiles in a way which makes me uncomfortable, like she knows something.

'He's such a handy man to have around, don't you think?' She shrugs on her coat and retrieves her bag from the counter.

'Yes, he is.' I am surprised when that appears to be it. She must be distracted by her upcoming appointment as she leaves moments later, and I breathe a sigh. The last thing I want is Sharon taking an interest in Ned and me. As I glance out of the window to watch her drive away, the sight of Amos letting himself into Manda Babcock's bungalow, with a key, catches my eye. *What the f*—? A word I often think but which never passes my lips. It is not expected from a sweet old lady.

The shop bell interrupts my thoughts as a gaggle of teenagers enters. They get my attention calling out greetings before they turn to meander up the aisles. All address me as Miss Smith remembering me from my time at the primary school. I might not have been on the teaching staff, but I was highly involved with many of the school activities, and I was a familiar face to everyone who attended. And I was a favourite with the pupils, even if I do say so myself, and this pays dividends now because they are all lovely to me. I suppose I went out of my way to involve myself with the children back then. When the school nurse was not around, I was always on hand to put my mothering instinct and energy into looking after all those with bumped heads or grazed knees. I do miss the children, but seeing them grow up through the awkward teenage years to become, hopefully, responsible adults is always such a tonic. It hit me a while ago, and with some sadness, that within only a couple more years none of the children at the primary school would remember me. It would not be long before there would be no more cheery hellos when they see me. How quickly time passes.

As I watch the group josh with each other it occurs to me that, as I do not have as many groups to attend or tasks to do in the village now, with Evelyn gone, I could perhaps volunteer some time at the school instead. My spirits lift at the thought and I cannot believe it has not come to me sooner. I decide to do something about this once I have sorted out the current situation with Amos because I would love to be back mothering the children again.

I keep an eye on the group as Sharon is not as tolerant and trusting of the youngsters as I am. But I cannot help glancing over towards Manda's house occasionally to see if there is any sign of Amos, or indeed Manda.

I cannot think why he would go into her house, and with what appears to be his own key. I had not seen Manda recently, and she had previously been a frequent visitor to the shop. Then I remember the conversation I had with Susannah Bugby at the funeral. She had said Manda had been suffering from agoraphobia since the row with Sharon. I wondered if Sharon was aware of the situation and if she had done anything about it. I suspected not, but perhaps offering an olive branch would help Manda. Olive branches were not exactly Sharon's thing, though.

Meanwhile, that did not explain why Amos was so keen on popping in. He certainly would not have been doing that if Evelyn was still alive. The shop door swings open as another customer enters, and I am chilled by the blast of cold air that hits me.

If Evelyn was still alive.

My thoughts jump to a conclusion I would rather they did not again, but I cannot think of any other explanation. It makes me distinctly uncomfortable that Amos could potentially be preying on these older, housebound women. Although as he has always portrayed himself to be a gentleman, it does not seem likely. But who can tell what gets into someone when their long-term partner has died? They might do all manner of things. Even so, the fact remains that I don't know what to do about the situation, other than continue to keep watch and perhaps gather some evidence of his wrongdoing. At least then I will have something to take to the police.

I feel the faintest shiver of excitement. Maybe, I might have finally caught him out doing something he should not.

Among other customers, Kyle Croxton calls in on his way home and I am reminded of my need to speak to him. He has a bunch of flowers in one hand and a large box of chocolates in the other by the time he gets to the till.

'Aww, is it Olivia's birthday?' I say, as I scan the items.

'No, it's an end of the week treat,' he grins as he reaches for his wallet.

'She is a lucky lady,' and I detect a hint of colour come to his cheeks.

'I think I'm the lucky one.' How lovely must it be to have someone feel like that about you?

'Actually, before you go, I have something to ask you.' His sandy eyebrows rise in anticipation. 'Are you and Olivia planning on going to the Murder Mystery at the end of the month?' I indicate towards the poster on the noticeboard advertising the event which this year is intriguingly called *The Poison Pen*.

'We were thinking about it, yes.'

'Brilliant. Would you like to join a table with me and Sally Button?' I put my hand out, fingers splayed. 'I realise you might have already made plans with other young people… but if you have not, we oldies would love to have you.'

'Sounds great. Thanks. That was one reason we were undecided, as we didn't know who we'd sit with. Who else is on the table besides you two?'

'I have not asked them yet, but we were going to invite Laura, Harry and Pip from The Stables. You know them, I assume?'

'Yes, of course. If you like, I'll ask them and let you know what they say?'

'That would be helpful. Thanks, Kyle.' As he walks away, I cannot help the wistful twist of envy which runs through me at how lovely it must be to have such a fine young man in love with you. I hope Olivia realises what a lucky woman she is.

Sharon is gone far longer than I expected. I suspect she has taken the opportunity of some free time away from the shop to do more than just have a doctor's appointment. It does not bother me that much, as I am keen to see how long Amos stays at Manda's place. A little under two hours, as it happens. I miss him opening the door, so do not catch a glimpse of Manda

46

seeing him off. If she was able to, of course, given her agoraphobia. But I see him closing the gate before walking as briskly as he can while still using a cane. I see he is also carrying a book. I was not sure if he had that with him when he entered or not and chastise myself for not noting such a detail.

Sharon returns a little after four.

'How did it go? You have been a long time,' I say, trying not to make it sound like an accusation.

'Sorry, yes. The actual appointment was over in a flash, you know what they're like, rushing you through. But then I had to wait around for some tests.'

'Oh, what sort?' I put my hands up. 'Sorry. If you would rather not say.'

'No, no. I know with you it won't go any further. Not like some. Just basic ones. Urine. Bloods. I even had an ECG.'

'Crikey, that sounds serious. What are they thinking is wrong?'

'I don't think they have any idea and are purely ruling things out. But he mentioned...' Sharon looks uncomfortable and glances round the shop to check we are alone, '... the menopause.' Those two words she mouths more than whispers. She is horrified at the thought, I can tell. 'I mean. I'm only forty.' She has a point, but I try to reassure her.

'The blood tests should tell them what is going on there, I imagine. Like you say, they are only ruling things out at this stage. Try not to worry.'

'You're probably right. It's hard not to, though. And they said to take it easier. So I might have to consider closing the shop a little earlier... unless...?' and she gazes at me with that look that tells me she wants something. As I realise what it is, I hold both hands up.

'Oh no, I cannot take on your evening shifts. I am sorry.' Her face falls, then quickly recovers.

'Then I shall just have to see if one of the other volunteers is more willing to help me out,' and as easily as that, I am left feeling like I am the bad guy.

'Good luck,' I say, determined to stick to my resolve as I collect my coat and am soon heading for home.

8: Getting Answers

Then

I travelled home with Dad in grim-faced silence. I had told him about the note, the gist of it, when I got back in. Held it clamped in my hand for the journey.

'Do you want to go find him?' he had asked. I had heard the hope in his voice. I think he would have liked to, even as we had driven home. If I had given the word, he would have turned the car around without hesitation. I could imagine him giving my fiancé, and I had to correct myself, my ex, a piece of his mind, maybe more than that, although I had never known my dad to be violent. I did not want him to get involved, or fight my battles for me.

'What is the point?' I had said. 'He no longer wants me. That is all there is to it.' My words made me sound tougher than I felt. But still, there was no future in chasing after a relationship that was no longer there.

Beth was still with Mum, who struggled to hold back tears when I told them what had happened. No need to say anything to anyone else. Word would gradually creep out. The truth was only what everyone thought, anyway. That he had jilted me.

I thanked Beth for staying with Mum and said she should get off now.

'Is there anything else I can do for you?' I shook my head. 'You know where I am if you need me.' I could see she was close to tears, never expecting today to end with such sadness. 'As soon as I get set up, I'll be in touch.' It was only then I was horribly reminded that she was leaving tomorrow. We had been going to spend a last joy-filled day together as a goodbye. But with everything, her leaving had slipped my mind. The fact I had forgotten was clear on my face.

'I am sorry, Beth. What must you think of me?' She smiled.

'Don't be ridiculous,' she said, and pulled me into a hug. 'It's been a terrible day and I wish I didn't have to go and leave you like this, but I'll be back for a visit before too long and I'll be in touch as soon as I'm settled.'

I shut myself in my bedroom before I cried. If I had started crying in front of my parents, it would have broken their hearts. But once the tears came, the release was extreme. I howled my disappointment and anger into a pillow. Punched it repeatedly. Furious thoughts whirled through my head and the adrenaline that flooded my body prevented me from sleeping. Eventually, I could lie in bed no longer and paced the floor like an enraged cat.

Uncle Jimmy had dropped off some food from The Snipe and Partridge earlier, but when Mum offered it to me, I could not eat a bite. Apparently, most of the guests had gone back to the pub. Naturally, there had been much speculation, but then they had eaten and drunk and gone home early. At some point I would have to write to them all to apologise for the expense they had gone to as well as the time they had wasted. But that would have to wait for another day because tonight I wanted to... I wanted to... I wanted to inflict damage. That was what I wanted. I wanted retaliation. I wanted vengeance. That was it. I wanted vengeance. None of these were good feelings, or even possible. But my plans to achieve them burned through my veins as the night wore on.

By dawn I was calmer. The fury that had consumed me was much reduced by my endless plotting, pacing and now, exhaustion.

As the sky lightened towards another beautiful day, my overriding feeling was that the way he had dumped me was the coward's way out. Although I couldn't change anything, I needed to see him so he could tell me to my face.

I thought through what I knew about my ex-fiancé, which didn't take long. Whereas before I thought he was someone who simply didn't talk much about himself or his life, now I suspected his reluctance to share was more about keeping it hidden. He was obviously not living at the flat where I thought he was and it occurred to me I did not know where he had lived before either. He had made out he was such a gentleman for not taking me back to his place which he referred to as his bedsit. When we met up, he would always meet me off the bus and we would go for a walk, or for fish and chips. We would often go to the cinema and occasionally to a dance in town, then he would walk me back to catch the late bus home.

He drove, but did not have a car. Although he had said he had borrowed one from a friend for the wedding as we had planned to go on our honeymoon in it. But now I did not know what to believe. Perhaps there was no car, and no friend. Although when I came to think about it, there was one. I had met him. Mick Archer. The best man. I knew even less about him.

I did have one lead I could follow. I knew where my ex worked. He had shown me on one of our walks. He was a brickie on an imposing building site in town. The post-war building boom ensured he would never be out of work, he had proudly

51

informed me. It was not likely he would have walked away from his job as well as me, and this gave me a place to start.

I spent the Sunday quietly and did little other than pack away my wedding dress and think. My parents and I pretended the atmosphere was not strained when we met up for meals.

On Monday morning I caught the bus into town and spent the journey ignoring the curious glances from fellow travellers from the village. I walked straight to the building site, assuming there would be an office where I could talk to someone. I did not even get past the gate. There was a ruddy-faced man with a clipboard on guard who reminded me of a bulldog my grandparents once had. I explained I was looking for someone, told him who, but his face remained blank.

'Never 'eard of 'im.'

'Is there someone else I can speak to?' I peered as far as I could through the gates to see if there was something resembling an office. I thought checking written records would be more thorough than simply relying on a trawl of someone's memory, but he was having none of it.

'I'm the site foreman, love. I know every man that works for the company. I have them down 'ere,' and he waggled his clipboard at me. 'Your fancy man 'as been pulling your leg, if 'e said 'e worked 'ere.'

A flush of embarrassment crept up my neck for being gullible enough to have believed everything I was told. I apologised for having wasted his time. He met my apology with little more than a grunt. As I walked away, I could not help but consider the possibility he was covering for my ex. My frustration grew at the thought, but I could not come up with a plan of how to get him to reveal what he knew. If that was anything at all.

I sat on a bench a little further down the road and kept an eye on the site entrance for a couple of hours. There was no sign of anyone I recognised.

When I had set off from home earlier, it had been with determination. Now, deflated, I had nowhere else to look. No other leads. If he was still in town, I daresay he was keeping his head down.

I wandered slowly up the High Street and thought about what I should do next. The only future I could see in front of me was to go home and get a job. Opening the door into a tearoom, I took a seat, looking out onto the road. I could not see there being a problem with my parents, but out of courtesy, I would need to check with them if it was all right for me to continue living with them. I decided I would do that as soon as I got back, and pushed away the crushing disappointment of not being on the brink of setting up my own home after all.

I stared out of the window as I sipped from my teacup. My life was going to be a lonely one with Beth gone as well as the husband I should have by now. As I wallowed in this realisation, a flash of flaming red hair caught my eye.

I grabbed my bag and rushed out of the door, keeping my eyes firmly fixed on the man walking on the pavement opposite. I checked the road for traffic and darted across when there was a break. I might have only met Mick Archer once, but the striking colour of his hair had stood out and now there he was. Despite him having his back to me, I was sure it was him. He had a long stride, and I struggled to keep up in my court shoes, having to break into a trot now and then to not lose ground. But he was clearly oblivious to the fact he was being followed, and I did not have to do anything other than keep him in sight. At the end of the High Street, and without breaking stride, he made

53

an abrupt right turn, swinging open the door to The Three Pitchers pub.

I had heard tales of how rough this pub was and had never gone into it myself because of its reputation. But that was not going to stop me today.

As confidently as Mick, I pushed the door open and walked into a poky bar several shades darker than the outside world. As I was clearly out of place, every eye turned in my direction. Mick was at the bar ordering a drink, observation not among his skills. Because it was not until the barman placed his pint on the bar, and jerked his chin in my direction, that he turned and realised what had silenced every other man in there.

'Shit,' was all he could muster by way of a greeting. Which only confirmed I had the right man.

'Where is he?' Uncomfortable in this alien and hostile environment, I jutted my chin out to look confident. His eyes darted around as though seeking an escape route, but I was between him and the only door I could see.

'You shouldn't be in here.'

'I am going nowhere until you tell me where he is.' No one in the dingy bar attempted to help or intervene, all apparently happy to watch the floor show.

Mick turned to the barman and told him he would be back for his drink, then he walked over and held the door open. 'Come on, we'll talk outside.'

Encouraged that I was about to get some answers, I followed him back onto the street and he led me round the corner where it was quieter.

'I don't know where he is.'

'Where does he work, because it is not at the site he showed me?'

'I don't know.'

'You don't know? How can you not know something like that when you are supposedly his best friend?'

'Well, you didn't know, and you were marrying him.' He held his hands up in defence immediately, and said, 'Sorry. That was a low blow,' then ran his fingers through his hair and walked back and forth, presumably struggling to make a decision.

'Just tell me what you know, Mick. I only want to understand what happened.'

He blurted out, 'I wasn't his best friend. Or even his friend. He was just someone I knew from the pub.' Another surprise.

'But you were his best man.' I was confused, but Mick merely shrugged.

'He told me he'd only moved to the area recently and his brother, who he would have asked, was working away and couldn't get here so he... er... he, er...'

'He what?' I chivvied him along.

Obviously uncomfortable, he struggled to look up from his shoes as he continued, 'He paid me to pretend to be his friend, and to be best man.'

'He paid you?'

'Yeah, he didn't want you worrying about him having no one to stand with him.'

'How thoughtful,' I said, but something unexpected occurred to me. 'He was originally intending on turning up then?'

'Of course.'

'But he met someone else before he could?'

'Yeah.'

'And were you there when that happened?'

'Er, no, not really.'

55

'Not really? Tell me.'

'He told me he'd just seen you for the last time before the big day and we went for a drink to talk through the arrangements for the wedding.'

'A drink? That night was meant to be his stag do.' More lies.

He shrugged, 'I know nothing about that. He was paying me so probably didn't have enough mates for a stag. Anyway, I had a date and only stayed for the one but I could see he fancied her.'

'Her?'

'The barmaid. I'd not seen her in there before.'

'Then you left him.'

'Yeah, because of my date.'

'Of course. Your date. Then what happened?'

'What do you mean?'

'He must have contacted you after that night?'

'He called me the next day and said the wedding was off, cos he'd met someone else.'

'Just like that.'

'Yeah, that's all he said.'

'Did he ask you to speak to me at all? Tell me the wedding was off?'

'No. Well, I assumed he'd have told you.'

'That would be a natural assumption.' My dry response made him realise the truth.

'Sorry. I can't believe he didn't. I would have done if I'd known. Honestly. But I wouldn't have a clue how to get in touch with you anyway.'

'Because you are not his real friend.'

'Exactly.'

'Do you know where he works?' Mick shook his head. 'What about the barmaid?'

'What about her?'

'I assume she was the woman who stole his heart so abruptly?'

'I guess so.'

'Do you know anything about her?' He shook his head again, then clearly had a thought.

'I know she was working in the pub that night—'

'Which pub?'

He raised his arm feebly in the direction of, 'The Bells, top of—'

'The High Street. I know where it is.' I sounded impatient, which only made him appear more uncomfortable.

'I'm sure I've seen her before though. Behind the counter of the post office.'

'The post office.' I take a moment. 'Thank you, Mick. You have been most helpful. You had best go and drink that pint. I think you need it.'

'I'm sorry.' He could not have looked more awkward if he tried, but I nodded at him and he escaped, I imagined with much relief.

I could not face going to the post office straight away. I needed to prepare for that, and for now I only wanted to go home, so I walked directly to the bus station with much to think about. Mostly, what flowed through my mind was how little I had known about my future husband and how utterly stupid I had been.

9: Coffee and Cake

Now

Alice Fraser knocks on the back door at eleven on the Saturday morning. She is my next-door neighbour and probably the closest thing I have to a best friend. We have much in common. Both of us are single and live alone – although not a cat in sight – but she is much younger than me, about to turn fifty – rather than a stone's throw away from seventy.

Fifty years. A generation apart.

She has worked for the same building company, Marchant & Son, her entire adult life, which I found extraordinary until she had once reminded me I had been a school secretary at the same school for the whole of my working life, too.

The thing is although we are friends; we are not confidantes – at least, she is not mine. Not that anyone else is either. I do not have anyone I can talk to about my concerns with Amos' recent behaviour. Everyone around here considers him beyond reproach. Although I consider saying something to her, I am hesitant because I don't want it to look like I am spying on him. Technically I am, but she does not need to know that. If she found out she would ask plenty of questions. She is not stupid.

Alice is a bit of a funny old thing. Not bad looking, but old before her time, in the way she dresses, although I noticed she substantially updated her work clothes a while back, and in her manner. I have suspected recently she is having a tough time at work. She does not say much, but her old boss died and since his son took over, something has changed. I have suggested she look for another job, but she seems reluctant. Mumbles on about

58

not finding something else at her time of life and with her lack of qualifications. I tell her experience counts for a lot, but she is not convinced. Confidence, that is what she lacks.

Actually, I think she was a bit in love with her old boss. Although I am one hundred percent sure nothing ever happened between them. She has always referred to him as Mr Marchant, which hardly speaks of an intimate relationship, does it.

She was married once, a long time ago, to George. He died in an accident at work. Alice became tearful at the recollection when she first told me, so I have never liked to ask anything more about it. Although a life wasted pining over a first husband seems a shame as there has been no romance since, other than possibly lusting after the boss, as far as Alice has said. There is certainly no Ned in her life to pop round for some light entertainment. Or maybe she simply has not confided as much in me. I can hardly blame her for that now, can I.

Anyway, we meet for coffee and cake most Saturdays, have chats over the adjoining wall when the weather allows, and are often to be found in our gardens in the summer months, enjoying a refreshing G&T or glass of wine.

I have already got the kettle on as I usher her in. We alternate on who hosts and usually she will arrive here with a dainty pastry or two. Today she places a plate bearing half a large butter-cream-iced and filled chocolate cake on my kitchen table before taking her usual seat. I consider where the rest of the cake has gone while, without asking if I want any, she cuts two substantial wedges. She slides them onto the side plates I had swiftly retrieved from the cupboard when she wielded the knife. I mean, I am never going to say no to chocolate cake, but everything in moderation.

By the time I turn with the mugs of coffee and sit, she is already well into her slice. It's too large to fit straight into her mouth, but she is at least using a fork.

'Is everything alright, Alice?'

'Had a terrible week.' She has barely cleared the last lot to utter these words before she forks another mouthful in.

'Sorry to hear that.' I pick up the knife to reduce my slice of cake to more manageable proportions. 'What has happened?'

'Young Mr Marchant. That's what.' It's a familiar cry. 'He's such... he's such...' She jabs her fork into the sponge as she struggles to find the right words. 'He's such an arrogant shit.' The fact she differentiates between the two Mr Marchants by prefacing their names with Young or Old never fails to make me smile.

'And cake is the answer?' She looks over at me and grimaces.

'I'm going to have to stop this, aren't I? I'll be the size of a house if I keep eating my emotions.' At least she has recognised the issue and, as I finish my first mouthful, I am relieved to see her push her plate away.

'I have told you before to leave.'

'I don't see why I should. I was there before him.' She etches petulance into every word as she gesticulates towards the remains of the cake, 'Can you put the rest of it in the freezer, take it to a coffee morning?' I nod and rise to remove the temptation from the table. I sense a certain amount of digging in of the heels on the job front, which is actually something else we have in common. The irony of me telling her to leave is not lost on me when that is exactly what I should have done many years ago, but we are both blessed with levels of tenacity that could rival the strongest-willed terrier.

60

'Maybe things will settle down in a bit,' I say in an attempt to give a little hope.

'Maybe. Something's going to have to change.' She sighs, then shakes her head as if to remove the thoughts she's having. She refocuses on me. 'Anyway, enough of that. How's your week been?' This is my cue to mention Amos's odd behaviour, but still something stops me from getting the words out.

Instead, I brush past the question with, 'Same old, same old.' And swiftly move on. 'Am I right in thinking you are part of the cast in the Murder Mystery?'

'Oh, yes. I'm quite looking forward to it. Amos has written this marvellous script. *The Poison Pen*. He's so clever. Well, he's got so much talent, of course. I'd never be able to come up with anything half as good.' I realise I was right not to mention his current pattern of behaviour. She'd never be able to see beyond how utterly brilliant he is.

But he is not that clever. He has never yet written a murder mystery I have not solved.

10: He Wasn't That Much of a Gentleman

Then

I realised I was pregnant six weeks later. The same week, my ex-fiancé married the other woman in a brief ceremony at the registry office. I watched them come and go from the other side of the street. Pushing the thorn deeper to keep the wound in my heart from healing.

He spotted me and I enjoyed his discomfort when he did, but, as a practised liar, he did not react in front of his new wife and the couple I took to be her parents. Instead, he hustled them along the pavement and, after a few hundred yards they entered a pub, no doubt to celebrate their nuptials. I left them in peace, knowing this was only the start.

I was too proud to make any sort of announcement of my condition to him. What could I expect him to do anyway? Support me? Leave his wife? If the love was not there, what would be the point?

I concentrated on finding out all I could about them instead. As well as being a part-time barmaid, she did indeed also work at the post office, industrious little bee that she was. I joined the queue to send a parcel occasionally to get a close-up look at her. She was attractive enough. Pretty, I supposed. More buxom than me and I suspected with a tendency to put on weight, something I had always kept in check. And she giggled. A lot. Her bubbly character, which was rather at odds with mine, did beg the question as to why he had ever been with me.

Still, she seemed sweet. It crossed my mind whether she had known about me. If she had purposely lured him away, or was the innocent party? I suspected the latter. What woman would do that to another? No, I was fairly certain she knew nothing of my existence, and wondered how long her new husband planned to keep it that way.

As if there was not enough misery in the house already over the cancelled wedding, and the guilt I carried about the money my parents had spent on it, I now had to deal another blow to the family.

I told Mum about the pregnancy first. I had to. I could not settle to anything; I could not seriously look for a job because I did not know what my future held. As it was, I think she had already guessed. I had kept catching her looking at me sideways and she did not seem as surprised by my news as I expected her to be. Her anxiety levels did increase though as soon as I confirmed she had something to be anxious about. She told Dad, gently and, bless him, he was nothing other than kind to me, but I could sense the tension in his stance, the set lines of his face. The same as on the wedding day when I knew he wanted to find my ex and give him a hard time.

I did not even get a lecture about my stupidity because, I assumed, they probably thought I had been through enough already.

Those were my parents, supportive and open-minded, but worriers, about me and about what this was going to do to me. Because there was no getting away from it. Living where we did, 1960s or not, having a baby out of wedlock was seen as a disgrace, and the ruin of a girl's reputation. We lived in a village in the countryside surrounding a small market town. Optimism and hedonism might be all the rage in London as whispers of the Swinging Sixties grew, but no one had seen so much as a miniskirt around here. There were many quick-to-the-altar weddings. Along with babies that came extraordinarily early.

In my case, a wedding was not an option.

When this happened, which it did, it being the stuff of hushed warnings and whispered gossip, families secreted their girls away to a distant relative who was possibly sick and in need of someone to help them get through their day-to-day lives. If they were lucky, they actually did stay with a relative. If they were not, a mother and baby home beckoned. Despite my parents being loving and supportive, my exile was to be no different because they did not want this to harm my future. When they talked to me, they used words like "my condition" or "this situation" and discussed the details in general terms because neither could bring themselves to use the word "baby".

Mum would have loved a large family, but it was not to be, me being the sole survivor of over a dozen pregnancies I was aware of. And I knew that what I was putting her through now was tearing her apart. Her pain was visible. Through the crack in her bedroom door, head bowed as she sat on the edge of the bed. The silent tears that fell as she did the washing up.

I knew, given half a chance, Mum would have accepted the child as her own with my baby being brought up as my sibling. I had heard stories of such things and it seemed like a way out. But if her age alone was not enough to make a pregnancy something akin to a miracle, sadly, her history was only too well known, her last unsuccessful pregnancy nearly being the death of her and resulting in an emergency operation which removed all the parts necessary to bear a child.

Exile it had to be, and adoption. Throughout this time, and out of respect, I held steadfast to the belief my parents were good people but at my age and at that time I had little say about the choices in my life. To my eternal shame I did not consider challenging them. I knew the decision to give away this grandchild was not taken lightly. And while they made it for all the right reasons, in their eyes, it would still have brought considerable stress and pain to their lives. I remained quiet, reflective, and suitably downcast. As I assumed they would expect me to be. What I failed to tell them, though, was how happy I was to be pregnant. How much I loved the changes in my body and how the thought of a whole new person growing inside thrilled me. I wish I had known then how much this failure to convey my feelings, wants, and desires would haunt me for the rest of my life.

Being of original Irish stock, my mother had no lack of relatives. I was sent to stay with my cousin Cara, who lived on a windswept croft on the west coast of Scotland. I had a certain trepidation about going because, despite living in a village, I knew nothing about farming. I was also worried Cara, who I had never met, would be a disapproving, fire-breathing dragon, who would preach hellfire and damnation on my soul for getting into such a predicament.

Mum and Dad waved me off at the station and I sensed their sadness. Mum was barely able to hold back her tears as she hugged me goodbye.

Nauseous for the entirety of the long, long, long journey. I wrote letters on the train. To my parents because they asked me to write weekly to let them know I was all right. I thought this first one could be yet another apology before I filled them in on what life with Cara was like; and to Beth, who was having a fabulous time in London and loving every moment of her life. I didn't share what had happened as I didn't want to worry her, merely mentioning that after the non-wedding I was going off to live with relatives for a while. If she read between the lines, I did not know. She never asked, and I never told. Sadly, my withholding of the truth put a barrier between us that had never been there before and that she was unaware of. I was not around for her first trips home and although we wrote it was all superficial news, at least from my side. Our once close relationship was hard to maintain via pen, paper and withheld truths. The time between letters inevitably lengthened. She sent condolences when my parents died and soon after she told me she had met someone, an American. By the time they married, our friendship did not warrant me being invited to the wedding. I did not mind. I could not face her by then. She had always been my confidante, and I knew I could not have seen her and not told her what had happened, so she was better off not knowing. Last thing I heard was she had gone off to live in America.

I stared out of the window, mesmerised by how different the scenery was the further north I travelled. After changing trains several times, when I finally reached my destination the insistent wind lowered the temperature by several degrees, whistling right through the thin coat I wore as I stepped down onto the platform. I was exhausted. I had no idea if the message had got through as to which train I would be on and, therefore, if anyone would be waiting for me.

I was also the only one to disembark at this rather isolated spot. There was a small station building, a road that led away, but no other properties, or people, in sight. Tired after the travelling and anxious over what I might be about to confront, I experienced a momentary panic, my heart fluttering in response, when I realised I did not know how to get in touch with, or find, Cara should she not turn up. And it was getting dark.

I walked out to the front of the station and, glad of its shelter, stood feeling a tad awkward with my case at my feet. I gazed round at the countryside before me, capturing what I could before it dissolved into the coming night. A bleak, beautiful landscape of tufted grass and rocky outcrops. A couple of lights too far in the distance to bring any comfort. The few trees stunted by the prevailing wind into misshapen claws pointed to the land that rose to craggy peaks on my right.

Within a couple of minutes, it was from that direction that the lights of a vehicle appeared a way off in the distance. As it slowly got closer, I could eventually see it was a farm truck with a cab up front and flatbed behind, although one that had sides to it, like a fence. It drew up in front of me and stopped with a squeal of brakes. A woman got out and grinned at me from the far side of the bonnet. She had a mass of curly, carrot-coloured hair which a scarf was making a valiant effort to control in the wind and she was wearing dungarees with a thick, checked jacket on top. I noted the muddy work boots she wore as she approached. 'You must be my cousin. You're the image of my aunt.' Her voice had a soft Irish lilt to it, her freckled face open. I was surprised by how young she was, and that she had any idea of what my mother looked like. As far as I was aware we had no photos of her family. Certainly, none had been shared with me. She took my hand and shook it vigorously before pulling me in for a hug. She exuded a strange kind of earthy scent, and I took to her immediately, attracted to her warmth.

'It is a pleasure to meet you, Cara.'

'Ahh, so formal, you make me feel ancient, and I'm only a few years older than you. Come on now, let's get going or it'll be dark before we get home.' I clambered up into the cab, the smell of oil hard to ignore, and we set off. A sheepdog, introduced as Jessie, happily panted on the seat between us. I glanced across at Cara, admiring her hair. It was much brighter than my mum's auburn, and mine, an ordinary brown, showed none of its vibrancy and was drably tame by comparison.

'It's a shame it's taken you getting knocked up for us to meet.' Initially shocked by how forthright she was, I was then relieved. It was nice to be with someone who was not going to pussyfoot around me, who would not talk about "my condition", with that last word whispered.

We met no other vehicles as we travelled along increasingly narrower lanes. I stared out of the window seeking quick glimpses of the distant sea as allowed by the failing light and the craggy countryside we passed through until we pulled into a rutted gap between stone walls and squelched to a stop in front of a gate.

'As a usual rule, the passenger opens it. But you hardly have the right footwear, so I'll let you off on this one and only occasion.' She glanced at the Mary Janes I wore and I cringed as she got out and lifted the gate across the muddy entrance. Having been born and brought up in a village, I thought I knew the countryside. I now appreciated how sanitised my existence had been and, already feeling out of my depth, I was apprehensive I would not have the right clothes for a place this wild and remote. Certainly, most of those in my case were utterly useless.

Within a couple of days, I knew being there was going to be alright as Cara opened my eyes. While nothing was said she was openly living with her "farm hand", Tom, who never appeared to go home to the house he apparently owned in the village. They lived in a small, one-storey, thatched stone cottage in need of much repair.

The front door opened into one room which had a range that required feeding with wood at the kitchen end, and a couple of saggy sofas covered in colourful knitted throws at the other. A well-scrubbed wooden table divided the two areas. Their bedroom led off the sitting room end. What was to be my room, the second bedroom, the kitchen end. It was tiny, for which Cara apologised, but it was perfectly adequate for my needs and I was thankful for it.

The toilet was nothing more than a seat over a bucket in a shed set a short way away from the cottage. The contents of the bucket had to be taken further from the property and tipped under a corrugated iron sheet. I was not sure of the process from there and not curious enough to find out more.

There was also a chamber pot under the bed for night-time use. I recognised it because we had had them when I was a child, before we had an indoor bathroom put in at home. Seeing it made me realise how much I had taken those facilities for granted.

Water was pumped from the well by hand. For washing it was warmed on the range then tipped into large jugs and carried back to our rooms. There I would pour the contents into a wide porcelain bowl, which Cara had beautifully decorated with flowers, and placed on the chest of drawers.

I went to bed that first night with mixed emotions. Home sickness prevailed but I could feel the faintest tinge of excitement at what I was going to experience there.

I would not be disappointed.

The next morning when I had gone outside it was like walking into another world. I had come from countryside but it was completely different to what faced me here. Back home was largely arable. Tamed fields surrounded our village. Crops grew and were harvested. Stock grazed in adequately fenced paddocks.

Here, I was greeted with a harsh wilderness by comparison. The croft was in the valley between two ranges of mountains. Although Tom told me they were little more than hills. Still the soft mounds of the hills back home were vastly different to the jagged rocks that had been forced out of the ground to make these.

A glittering ribbon could be seen on the horizon where sea divided earth and sky. And excitement bubbled up inside me, to be this close to it. I could not wait to walk out to see if there was a beach.

Stone walls divided areas on the croft. Cara had a few Highland cattle and was building her herd. But the majority of her stock were sheep and I could see them dotted on the hillsides.

I was happy to work on the croft while I was there as well as preparing meals to free up Cara and Tom's time. Cara also helped me out of my clothing crisis by lending me some of hers, and as I grew larger, we became creative with Tom's clothes too. If anyone from home had visited, they would never have recognised me as I spent every day in shabby work gear. Unlike at home, I did not care what I looked like as there was no one around to see me and I could just be comfortable.

Leaving aside the looming emotional issue I was going to have to confront, I genuinely had some of the best and most liberated days of my life there.

Before I left home, my parents and I had agreed, once the baby was born, I would put her up for adoption. But I had decided one thing myself, I had until my baby arrived to spend time with her, and that is what I did.

I talked to her all the time. I said her because, despite being pregnant at a time before you could find out the sex of your baby, I knew I was carrying a girl. Picturing her clearly with dark hair like mine, I chatted to her all day long as I went about my chores. I told her of the situation I had found myself in. That it was not one of my making as she should have been born into a loving marriage, but that her feckless father had had a last-minute change of heart. I explained about the humiliation of being left at the altar, and of the ultimate joy of finding she was on the way. I told her I would have kept her if I could but I would have no opportunity to provide for her on my own. We sadly lived in a time when it was considered a disgrace to have a child out of wedlock and I could not let myself and my baby be an embarrassment for my parents. I also did not want her gossiped about or marked out as different by the judgement of others who only cared about appearances while sweeping their own dirty little secrets under the rug. I told her I loved her; I would always love her. I was sure she would have a loving home to grow up in and a family who could provide for her in a way that was not possible for me. But if she ever wanted to find me in the future, she could and I would welcome her with open arms.

Rosie, I named her.

Cara caught me talking to her and suggested I stop.

'You're getting too close,' she said. 'It will only make the eventual parting harder.'

'How can talking to her make me any closer than we are already?' I said, while my hand rested on my bump where it could feel her moving beneath it.

Cara had no answer. She simply shrugged and shook her head. But I caught the worried expression that crossed her face whenever she looked at me, and suspected she regretted taking me in.

My mind often drifted to my parents, and I thought about where their emotions were regarding their grandchild. Did they even think of her as that, or had they blocked any such thoughts? While I tried not to, as time went on I could not help my feelings towards them hardening when I considered that what they had done amounted to the abandonment of their grandchild.

Of course, while my parents had disappointed me, the person I blamed entirely for my situation was my ex. Not so gentlemanly after all, as it turned out. I tried not to think of him in his new life with his new wife because it ruined the time I had with Rosie. But there was no getting away from the fact I was having to give her up because of him, and that was hard to forgive. Once I had firmly laid the blame at his door, I pushed all other thoughts of him from my mind whenever they appeared. They would keep for another day.

I had never wanted a winter to pass so slowly. Determined to do my bit on the croft, I would be out at first light to break the ice on all the troughs. I would make my way carefully across treacherous paths whose frozen ruts were hazards primed to twist an ankle. Others slick with ice patches I had to take great care crossing for fear of falling. Wrapped up warmly, I thankfully wore an old coat Tom had offered me. But my woollen gloves were no match for the icy wind that whipped in off the sea and bit into my fingers and face.

Cara and Tom wanted me to slow down as my time drew near, but I would not. Accompanied by Jessie when she was not working elsewhere, I spent as much time as I could otherwise alone with Rosie. I told her of all the things I had wanted to do with her. The walks we would have gone on, the picnics, the fairs I would have taken her to, the pets we would have had. As the days gradually grew longer, I became more animated in my discussions with her. I chatted about what she might become, whether she would be a scientist or creative, musical or artistic. I told her all I had ever wanted to be was a mother, a grandmother, but that she could be anything she set her mind to and she always had to remember that.

The first pain tightened my stomach when I was at the furthermost point on the croft. In sight of the white sand on the beach, the cramping came and went like the waves on the shoreline. My pulse quickened in reaction as Jessie drew near. I had finished checking on the stock there anyway, so started my journey back to the cottage. The next contraction came a couple of minutes later, stronger than the first. Strong enough to take my breath away. It caused me to pause for its duration while I steadied myself, one hand on the stone wall that ran away into the hills. Having experienced practice contractions for a few weeks, I had not been sure if I would be able to tell when the real thing began. But there was no mistaking the difference.

My progress back to the cottage was slow. Jessie, anxious, ran ahead then turned back and whined on her return to me. I had to stop as each contraction began, needing the world to pause around me. There was no fear, just anticipation I was going to see Rosie for the first time. That I was finally going to meet my baby. I would not allow myself to think beyond that moment.

Cara spotted me first. I was deep, deep, deep into a contraction as she came round the corner of one field and found me doubled over and trying to control my breathing. I heard her call for Tom, tell him to bring the truck. The shock of the gush of warm liquid from between my legs prevented me from moving further. Moments later, they were both with me, carefully helping me into the cab. I had arranged to have my baby in the hospital. Most births were there in those days, and it seemed the safest option. Plus, I thought it would be easier with the adoption process, but now I was not sure. I did not relish the harsh, bumpy journey ahead in the truck and I considered staying put. It would be easier and more comfortable to have Rosie by the fireside and then live there forever, just her and me. All this whirled in my head but I was too far gone to voice my change of plan.

Later, when I remembered these thoughts, I knew they were simply a fanciful delusion of an impossible life. Money was hard to come by on the croft. Barely enough to keep Cara and Tom, let alone two more mouths. I knew Mum and Dad had paid Cara something for having me and that would not continue indefinitely, especially if I did not stick to my side of the bargain. I also loved Cara and Tom by then and did not want to be a burden on them any more than I wanted to be one for my parents.

I was glad Tom and Cara had come to my rescue. That they scooped me up and followed the plan we had made. Fanciful notions aside, I am a practical person. I knew what made sense, but my heart was breaking, even then.

Cara had always said it would be a challenge to get me to the hospital in time for the birth. It was an hour away, and I spent every minute thinking with each contraction that this was it. Rosie was going to be born in the cab of a farm truck. Cara calmed me with soothing words as best she could while she drove as quickly as possible, given the size of the roads and the state of them. Each rut and pothole jarred my already fragile body.

There was no telephone at the croft, so they could not call ahead and let staff at the hospital know I was on my way. Cara pulled straight up to the main doors, and Tom leapt off the flat bed of the truck to help me out. I could sense his relief as he got me into a wheelchair and left me with Cara at the entrance. The plan was for him to take the truck home and get caught up with the farm jobs, then come back once it was dark to see how things were going.

Cara pushed me into the hospital and got me to the maternity department. I was unaware of my surroundings as wave after wave of contractions hit me with barely a break in between to gather myself. Struggling to catch my breath I was relieved when two midwives approached and moments later, I was on a bed, being examined. Cara told them who I was, what had happened, and all the while she held on to my hand, which I gripped like a vice. The pain was intense and all-consuming, but primeval forces had taken over and my body knew what it was doing. One midwife told me to let her know when I wanted to push as she prepared at the other end of the room. Apron donned. Hands scrubbed. I thought the birth would be hours away yet. All I had read had prepared me for a long labour but on the next wave there was a definite change to the feel of the contraction and I had no option but to bear down as nature took over. Unable to speak, I heard Cara tell the midwife I was pushing, and she rushed to the end of the bed. On the next wave, the pain climbed to a crescendo I thought would never end. Eventually it reached a peak that made me want to scream if only I had had the breath to do so, and the midwife told me the head was out. The worst was over. She was right, two more contractions and Rosie was born.

'A beautiful little girl,' Cara smiled down at me, as she wiped away tears that streamed down her face. They placed Rosie on my chest and I adjusted my clothing, opening my top until we were skin to skin. She smelled so good and I was overcome with relief now the pain had subsided. Another small contraction came as I passed the afterbirth, and that was it. My body relaxed. Rosie was taken from me briefly while they did a few tests.

The midwife said, 'Do you want to hold her again?' They knew the score; they knew I was not keeping her and apparently many mothers in my situation found it easier not to have ever held their babies. There was no way I could do that. I intended treasuring every second I had with her.

'Yes,' I said, and held my arms out ready. The midwife smiled. Later, she told me I made the right choice. Mothers who interacted with their babies found it easier to move on after they had given them up for adoption, but I found that difficult to believe. Even then I knew that when the Rosie-shaped piece of my heart was torn away, I would never recover.

Rosie was perfect. When I held her, she stared at me solemnly out of the biggest, bluest eyes I had ever seen. She had a lot of dark hair which stuck up in tufts, and a rosebud mouth, the sort I had only ever previously encountered in books. I could not stop gazing at her and taking in every inch of her beauty.

Cara stayed with me until Tom returned. I offered her baby cuddles. Then was surprised to see tears come again once she had Rosie in her arms.

'Cara?' I met her eyes and recognised the truth. She had been here. She had done this. 'Why didn't you say?'

'I can't talk about it. It's still too painful, even after all these years.'

'Yet you agreed to take me in and put yourself through this. Why?'

'I thought it would be alright and, to be honest, it was right up until this bit.' She pasted on a smile, but there was desperate sadness behind it. I couldn't believe I had never noticed, but suspected it only became visible once I had shared her experience.

'Do you want to tell me about your baby?' She shook her head.

'Not now, maybe later. For now, you need to concentrate on Rosie here. Everything else can wait.' She helped me get cleaned up and into a fresh nightdress, then they took me to a ward full of mothers and their new babies. I drew a curtain around the bed to cocoon us from the world while Rosie and I got to know each other. I was told I could bathe her in the morning.

When Rosie started mewling, another midwife popped her head round the curtain and asked if I wanted to feed her or would I rather she be put on the bottle. I was determined to experience everything I could, and wanted to try to breastfeed her. Her rosebud mouth automatically started seeking sustenance as soon as she was near my nipple and latching on was no problem. The midwife smiled and said, 'You have an easy baby. Not all take to it as quickly.' Her words made me ridiculously proud of how clever my baby was. Once Rosie had finished, the midwife came back to show me how to change her nappy, folding the terry towelling cloth until it fitted around Rosie's tiny bottom. I wondered if Rosie knew how short our time was together, if she was making the best of it like me. I had told her, of course, over the last few months.

Tom came to see how things were going early evening. Surprised to find Rosie had already arrived, he studied Cara closely. He knew.

Rosie was born on the twenty-ninth of March. I got to be with her for twenty-four hours. They turned out to be the best twenty-four hours of my life.

The next day, the day I had to leave her at the hospital, was the worst. It was the most unnatural, traumatic thing I have ever experienced and I have never recovered from it.

A day has not passed since that my arms have not ached from the emptiness.

I spent a couple of weeks recovering on the croft. Cara fussed around me in a way she had not leading up to the birth and I knew now her own experience coloured this. The physical wounds of the delivery gradually healed. A process I hated because as each day passed, each improvement took me further away from Rosie. The emotional pain, however, remained imprinted on my broken heart, the hurt ground in deep as though cut with glass, a constant reminder of what I had done.

To get through the days, I started light chores around the croft to busy my mind and contribute. Cara and Tom were kind enough to say they would miss my input once I was gone. To get through the nights, I sobbed into my pillow and each morning woke bleary-eyed and with it held tight in my arms as though I was clinging to a lifebuoy.

The day before I was due to leave, Cara and I took a walk out to the sea. It was a beautiful April day. The sun was out, the breeze light. During my recovery, Cara had eventually told me a little about her baby and she had had a much worse time than me. Back in Ireland the priest in her village had driven her out once her pregnancy was known. She was sent to a terrible mother and baby home where the adoption of her baby had been forced upon her as she was unmarried and therefore seen as unfit to have a child. Apparently, it was common practice in Ireland and I could not think of anything more horrific. At least I had had some say, made some decision, even if that decision was out of my hands. I had asked if her family had supported her or helped in any way but, afraid of gossip, her family had done nothing to stop the priest. Although, as she related, priests held a terrible power over communities and there was little they could have done.

Despite her defending her family, I sensed a chasm had developed between them. Certainly, there had been no contact that I was aware of since I had been living there.

As we walked along a beach of the whitest sand I had ever seen, I said, 'It was bad enough to leave Rosie in the hospital. I cannot bear the thought of her being in an entirely different country to me.'

'Don't dwell on the thought you have abandoned her, Dora. No good will come of it. Instead, focus on the fact you have made a family. I found it's the only way you can think of it, otherwise you will drive yourself mad.' Those are probably the wisest words anyone has ever said to me. I clung to them then and have carried them in my heart ever since.

By the time I left, we were good friends. Cara, Tom and I. Although I suspected they would be pleased to have the place to themselves again, for me we were bound forever by an experience.

I stayed in touch with them, another pen-pal arrangement like with Beth, but this one lasted. I heard when they sneaked off to Gretna to tie the knot. Just them. Two passing strangers as witnesses. A year or so later, Cara delighted me with the news a baby was on the way. While I had every intention of travelling to Scotland whenever I could, when it came to it, I couldn't face it. The memories. The unbearable thought I was closer to Rosie yet still unable to see her, to be with her. It was too much. Cara understood. She understood everything. We never met again.

She is three years older than me; Tom is still by her side, just turned seventy-five, and they have two children and five grandchildren. All with flaming red hair. She sends photos every Christmas, and I cry at her joy.

I returned home a different person. Destined to be forever lonely without my little girl, I got a job in a local law firm typing letters and wills and all manner of legal paperwork. It was mind-numbingly boring. But it suited my purpose, which was to be working in town. That way I could spend each lunch time keeping tabs on my least favourite people. I supposed I knew right back then I was building an unhealthy obsession, but I did not care. I could not stop and did not want to.

She was still working in the post office and I would pop in there when the need arose, always careful not to become too familiar. He, I eventually found, was working on a new block of flats, although he was now the one with the clipboard, which was an interesting development.

I had not found out where they were living, yet.

Each night I stayed in. I had no desire to socialise or, as my parents put it, "get back to normal." That option no longer existed.

They never asked one single question about what I had been through, or the most important person in my life. That was what hurt the most. The lack of interest in their grandchild. It created a wall between us that stifled conversations. Words checked and considered before they left mouths.

I knew they worried and, now a parent myself, I had more empathy for their concerns but could do little to assuage their feelings. A tension grew which had not been there before and I did not know how to convince them I was alright enough to put their minds at rest when I was not alright at all, but then, one day, everything changed.

Dad died. Suddenly. At work.

One moment he was alive, the next, not.

My parents were older than those of many I knew of my age because it had taken so long for me to arrive. But they were still relatively young. Not even retired yet.

The shock hit Mum terribly.

Having married her school sweetheart, she faded from that moment on. A broken heart, she told me. The half she had given to my dad was missing, and what was left incapable of sustaining her. She did not last another six months.

As she weakened, she kept apologising. There was no elaboration but we both knew what for. I said I forgave her but she did not believe me. Her last words hoarse and strained as I held her hand in the cottage hospital were still, 'I'm sorry.'

I didn't believe me either.

And I don't believe she ever forgave herself.

I settled their affairs and put the house on the market, the place too big for me alone. With no clear focus on what I should do next. It was the right time for a complete change, and for a while I mulled over moving to Scotland. But with no idea where Rosie might be, I hadn't a clue where best to live. It was at that point fate intervened. I had my parents' property on the market with an estate agency in town. One day, as I approached that agency for an update, I saw my ex and his delightful wife exiting. As I entered, the agent was still collecting together the property details I assumed they had been viewing. A pretty cottage in a village. I picked up the sheet from his desk.

'Oh, this is exactly what I am looking for.'

The agent smiled at me and said, 'I'm sorry, but it's already gone. The vendors have just accepted an offer for it. You narrowly missed the purchasers leaving.'

'What a shame. It is lovely.'

'We have other cottages, if you're interested. And, in fact, we have another one in the same village which has recently come onto the market.' He reached into a filing cabinet and pulled out the particulars. 'It's a smaller property. Already vacant.'

I viewed it the following day. The cottage was built of beautiful stone and as soon as I walked in, I was home. But the agent was right. It was small. There was a sitting room and kitchen downstairs. Two bedrooms and a bathroom up. The rooms were of a good size though. The kitchen large enough to take a table, and having a bay window in the sitting room made all the difference. There was also a long back garden to keep me busy.

Also it could not have been more perfectly positioned. The vendors accepted my offer, and I entered the tortuous process of simultaneously selling one property while buying another. It took months during which I fretted about the chain below me collapsing and me losing the cottage I had set my heart on.

11: We Meet Again

Then

It was 2 years, 106 days since I last saw Rosie.

The look on my ex's face when he spotted me the morning after I moved in was priceless. I was out at my car getting a few things in when he walked down the narrow pathway between his cottage and the one next door. The cottages were connected on the first floor, but at ground level a channel had been burrowed out between the two for access to the rear gardens. There was the same set-up on my side, one of these passageways every two houses. He reached the pavement and looked like he was about to turn toward the shop when he glanced over and did a double take.

'You!' he said.

'Me.' I added a smile. Waited to see if he would approach. He did. Quickly checking both ways first.

'What are you doing here?' He was cross, which was not terribly neighbourly.

'I live here.' I did a half-turn with my upper body to indicate to my cottage behind me.

'You can't.' I loved his outrage. Hoped his wife would get the chance to hear it. I could see her approaching over his shoulder.

'Oh, but I can.'

'There you are,' called the wife, sadly before she was near enough to hear the tension in his words. He had only been gone a few seconds though. She certainly kept her eye on him, which was interesting. His face dropped; a smile replaced the frown before he turned to his wife.

'Hi, darling. I'm meeting our new neighbour.' He slipped an arm around her waist, pulled her to him to make it absolutely, positively clear to me just how married he was. 'I'm sorry we haven't got as far as names. I'm Amos and this is my wife, Evelyn.' *Oh, playing that game, are we?* I smiled sweetly at Evelyn.

'How lovely to meet you. I am Dora. I was telling your husband I moved in last night. Not that I have many things to actually move in.' I laughed lightly. 'I am planning on decorating the place first and doing up the rooms as I go.'

'That's a good idea. We did much the same. Only moved in a few months ago ourselves.'

'From what I can see, your cottage looks wonderfully homely. You must have worked terribly hard on it.' Evelyn beamed with pride and gazed with adoring eyes at Amos.

'It was all him. All the hard work, anyway. I did the soft furnishings. You'll have to come over and have a proper look round one day.' Amos cleared his throat as though something jagged had lodged itself in there.

'I would love that.' I gazed at her. There was something about her, something I could not quite put my finger on.

'I'm sure Amos would be delighted to help you out if you need anything doing. Although...' and she smiled up at him again '... he will be busy for a while as we need another room decorating now.' Her hand dropped to her stomach. And there it was. The something. The baby on the way that changed everything. I had thought of a hundred ways this first meeting would go, but had never considered that possibility. My stomach turned over, bile in my mouth as I struggled to maintain my composure and plaster a smile on my face.

'Oh, congratulations. How exciting for you both and that is a kind offer, thank you. Good at decorating, are you? I may take you up on it,' and I attempted to look gratefully at Amos, who scowled at me.

Evelyn was looking around as if searching for something, or someone.

'Are you, er… I mean, is there… anyone else moving in with you?' she continued, prying.

'No, no, it's only me.'

'Ah. How independent of you,' she checked her watch, 'you must excuse me, I have to get ready for work.'

'Nice to meet you, Evelyn.' I half expected Amos to turn away with her, but he did not. He started telling me when the bins were emptied, like I would be interested, moving on to details about the milk round, all an excuse to carry on chatting until she was back in the house. His mask fell again.

'Is this a coincidence? You moving here?'

'Of course not. Where would be the fun in that?'

'Some sort of revenge then. Is that what you're after? Or an apology?'

'That would be nice. If far too late. A note, Amos. Was that all I was worth?' I was delighted to see the flush spread up his face. 'Actually, don't bother answering. I am more intrigued by the fact you did not tell your wife we knew each other.'

'I didn't want all that business coming out.'

I nodded, as though I understood, 'All that business… no, I imagine you would not want that coming out. It would not be right, would it? Not for a fine upstanding gentleman like yourself.'

'Look, what is it you want? What are you going to do or say?' He glanced anxiously over his shoulder in case Evelyn should make a reappearance.

And that was the big question. What did I want? Because I was not entirely sure myself. I had played many scenarios through my mind without ever reaching a conclusion that had fully satisfied me. Thinking I would know what I wanted once we met again, I had left it to my physical and emotional reaction to guide me. I had to admit I had been on the cusp of revealing our past connection to Evelyn, to cause some disruption which would have no doubt eventually opened up the door to me telling him about Rosie. But one tiny movement had changed all that, Evelyn's hand on her stomach. I remembered doing the same. Right at the beginning, where Evelyn was now, when there was nothing to see and it seemed unbelievable a life could be developing inside. Then later when you could feel the baby twist and turn, kick, punch and stretch.

Much as I wanted to stir things up for Amos, as a parent now myself it felt unfair to deliberately cause trouble and inflict any potential marital unrest on an innocent baby.

'We'll have to move,' he said, almost to himself.

I smiled, because despite my softening heart, I was not going to let him off that lightly. 'You can try. But I found you once and I will find you again.' Baby or no baby, I was not going away that easily and I could still wind him up. An expression crossed his face that was hard to fathom, so I changed tack. 'Anyway, have you had a turn-up in your fortunes? A cottage in the countryside is a jump up from our little rented flat in town. How do you afford it on a brickie's pay?' I frowned as I looked him up and down, not giving away the fact I already knew he had had a change in circumstances. 'Now I come to think about it you are hardly dressed for a day on site.' He looked uncomfortable, shifted his feet.

'I work in the office now. Different construction firm.'

'Do you? That is a quick rise.'

He cleared his throat. 'Evelyn's father took me on.' I smiled as the penny dropped. She came from somewhere higher on the social scale than us. I had suspected as much. Could tell by the clothes she wore. Not overly expensive, but nothing cheap. I could not help but be impressed by the fact she worked hard too. Did not just live off daddy, although perhaps that was because they were not so far above us after all, the construction firm maybe only a small company.

'Of course he did. Nothing quite like nepotism, is there. And now you are providing them with a grandchild to cement the relationship.' The cynical side of me could not help but wonder exactly when he had found out what Evelyn's father did for a living.

'They're delighted. Anyway, you've done alright for yourself too.' He gesticulated towards my cottage to direct the focus onto me.

'My parents died.' He went to speak. I cut him off, not wanting to hear whatever he was about to say. 'Stress. That is what killed them.' And I fixed him with a look fit to shatter glass.

There was little he could say in response, so he excused himself and left for work. I got on with my day, pleased to get through the first meeting and for it to be confirmed that after everything that had happened, I was no longer attracted to him. Although I had thought I had worked through my feelings for him while on the croft, I had not been sure how it would be to see him again and it was a relief to discover any feelings I had ever had for him had vanished.

He kept the deception of our previous relationship from Evelyn for a few months. But I think the pressure of wondering if the axe was about to fall with me revealing the past finally got too much. Evelyn and I had become, if not friends, certainly good acquaintances, and I thought he only told her for fear we would get too close. I might even have started coming to their house and he would not have stood for that. Naturally, he therefore had to warn her off me.

He chose to tell her the truth as the birth approached. Maybe he needed to clear his conscience before this momentous change in his life. I do not know. Anyway, I imagined half the village heard the ensuing row. And while I had not known at the time what it was about, he told me the next day when we were both about to get in our cars to go to work that I had nothing over him now. Not that I had exactly been waving it around as a threat, but clearly, he had succumbed to the pressure of it hanging there like the sword of Damocles. Anyway, she now knew it all, apparently, and for a while she gave me the cold shoulder, which suited me fine. Then one day I heard they had had a girl. I put on a happy face for them, although my heart twisted when people told me what an adoring father Amos was.

A few weeks later, Evelyn called me over as she pushed the pram out of the gate. The last thing I wanted to do was look at her baby, dreading seeing Rosie in her.

She told me she was sorry for ignoring me, but Amos had taken her by surprise with the news of our previous relationship. And she was none too pleased with him. They had had words, and things had been difficult between them for a while. I felt no guilt at the thrill of pleasure this gave me.

'Please believe me, Dora, when I say I had no idea he was about to get married when we met. I'm sorry.' I believed her. She seemed genuine in her apology. It was a shame she did not leave it there because she followed it up with, 'Although I'm sure you'll agree I make him far happier than you would have been able to. Anyway, I'm choosing to forgive you.' Which was big of her, although for what I was not entirely sure, and at the time I had been so taken aback by her previous comment I did not ask. I simply nodded instead as I peered into the pram and saw a face only a mother could love. My relief overrode any need to question her forgiveness and I let it lie. Although she could not quite let it go, ending the one-sided conversation with, 'There's no need for anyone else to know though, is there.' This was not said as a question. However, being jilted was not something I particularly wanted spread around either. Amazingly for a village, or perhaps not, given the desire for the three of us to keep it under wraps, as far as I am aware no one else knows about us. It is our little secret. But while Evelyn never made a public thing of it, privately she never missed an opportunity to have a little dig.

When I was building up to the move to Melton, my original plan on seeing Amos again had been to tell him about Rosie. I had had every intention of doing so, but when the time came, the words would not come out, and from the moment I knew there was a baby on the way for them, there was never a right time. Maybe I was a coward. Or maybe I was bitter at how much he doted on his children. But as time went on and in due course a second daughter joined the first, I rationalised my keeping Rosie a secret by deciding he did not deserve to know she even existed. If our past was to be a secret from the village, then she was a secret only I would know.

Of course, what I should have done as soon as I met them again was move. Immediately. That would have been the healthy thing to do. I was not sure what it was I was after or how I thought living this close to them might help because I had dealt with my feelings towards Amos while living on the croft and was over the jilting. I had also moved on from the shame and disappointment of part of my life falling apart. It was the fact I had had to give up my daughter because of his behaviour that I found impossibly hard to forgive. Or move on past.

Also, I had settled into Melton quickly, so why should I leave? I loved my cottage. My job at the school and meeting new people in Melton was easy because everyone saw me for exactly what I appeared to be; a young, single woman setting up home and starting a new job. I was far too young for people to expect me to have had any sort of past. No one would have considered being jilted and giving up a child for adoption were things that could have already happened to me. No one here asked if I had children because they knew me. Or assumed they did. Besides, I was not married therefore I could not have had children. No one thought beyond that fact. Whereas, as time passed and more than once I had considered moving on, it would have involved meeting new people. I knew at some point someone would ask if I had had children and the thought of denying Rosie's existence made my heart physically ache. In polite society though, people never expect you to respond with, 'Oh, yes, I have a wonderful daughter I love with all my heart but I gave up her up for adoption.' That was not the done thing at all and would put a right dampener on a conversation.

It was bad enough seeing the surrounding families grow over the years as I gave up on my dreams. Watching women just like me become mothers, then grandmothers.

Amos and Evelyn remained acquaintances. Although he distanced himself more than she did, speaking to me only when it was unavoidable. We interacted at the school where I got to see their girls grow up, and in the village. But I never went into their house. We were not as close as friends. Amos saw to that.

Instead, they became the people I probably knew most about, becoming hyper aware of every little thing they did. Over the years, I watched the detailed routines of their lives along with the bigger picture; the working years, the children growing up, the empty nest and retirement.

It had surprised me they had not moved. I know what I said when we first met again but still it had been something I had expected them to do. As time moved on though, the money and prospects he had perhaps expected working for the family firm had not materialised and it appeared all was not well within the family. After doing a little digging when his father-in-law retired, I found out Amos and Evelyn had not been left the company as I assumed they would be. Indeed, it had been sold elsewhere which led me to believe Amos' expectations had not been met. Or perhaps Amos had not met those of his father-in-law.

Throughout those years, I became involved in village activities. If you live in a village, you will know what I mean by these, and having had the upbringing I had had, getting involved with the community was ingrained in me. Having said that, my first involvement actually came along because of my role as school secretary. One of the school governors approached me as there was a vacancy for the position of clerk to the Parish Council of Melton and asked if I would be interested. I wasn't particularly, but I thought it might be a useful position to be in. I would get to know some of those who took part in this lowest level of government as councillors and find out what was going on in the village, too. The plus being that the role was one step removed from being a parish councillor which suited me fine.

Discovering Amos Chamberlain was one of the parish councillors also triggered something in me. Particularly when he barely concealed his disapproval at my appointment. Realising this irked him only spurred me on to take the job, and in hindsight I know this was the turning point in my obsession with the couple.

I went along to the church they frequented but, unlike my parents who clearly had more faith than me, I stayed on the periphery. While I was happy to attend services and occasionally take the collection or read a lesson, try as they might the elders of village life could not involve me in making cross-stitch kneelers or any organisational duties. Although I did join the flower rota, but only because I heard Evelyn was on it. Of course, I could always claim work as being my excuse for not doing anything I did not want to as back then women rarely worked outside the home, especially once they had had children. Supposedly, stay-at-home mothers had more free time to give to the community than a woman with a job. Which did not seem at all likely to me.

Over time, the activities run in the village changed and developed as popular and less popular events came and went. In my first few years there, I was mostly involved with the fundraising efforts for the renovation of the village hall. I baked for many coffee mornings, although could rarely attend because of work, helped run quiz nights and organised discos for the youngsters in the village.

Amos, Evelyn and I ended up interacting in all manner of village activities because they were joiners and loved to be involved in village life. I was less inclined to be part of many of the activities they were doing, but by now it was my duty. If only to irk them. If I found out they had joined a group, so did I and they rarely had a break from me. Petty, but that is how it was.

Over the years, we had therefore been involved in many, many groups. While Evelyn excelled in all needlework activities, I was most challenged by the Crafty Meltonites, whose more inclusive activities covered knitting, crochet, sewing and embroidery and should not be confused with the more hard-core Quilters, of which we were also members. I never managed to put together a quilt and instead spent most of the afternoon sessions making refreshments for the dedicated. When Evelyn died and, with some relief, I left both groups due to my lack of crafting skill, not that such a minor detail had prevented me from attending for years, and strangely neither had it ever been commented upon by anyone. In addition, there was Games Club, indoor bowls (a great attraction for retirees), yoga and Pilates sessions, Cinema Club, Book Club and Writers' Group. Thankfully, Amos and Evelyn were not sporty, so I did not have to involve myself in football, cricket, tennis, hockey, or basketball on the playing field. The village hall committee of which we were all part, organised banquets, quiz nights, bingo and a whole range of other community events; including my personal favourite, the Murder Mystery evening. Amos and Evelyn were natural stars of the show in M.A.T.S. (Melton Amateur Theatrical Society) whereas I was happy to be front of house. In more recent years, Vinyl Club and a Sign Language Course had kept us busy.

In short, I appeared wherever Amos and Evelyn were and became the irritation they simply could not get rid of.

12: Fate Had Plenty to Answer For

Then

It was 29 years, 264 days since I last saw Rosie.

Years later, at the Christmas do for the book club we both belonged to I found out how they met. During the meal, it came up that it had been their thirtieth wedding anniversary that year, which came as no surprise to me, but I bit back the question I had wanted to know the answer to throughout every one of those years. Thankfully, Susannah Bugby took the opportunity to ask how they met and I could have hugged her for it. As I had finished eating, I sat back to listen and focused on Evelyn, who was diagonally opposite me.

'Oh, it was a whirlwind,' she said. 'His local pub was unexpectedly closed, burst pipe or broken boiler, something like that.' She paused for a moment as though trying to recall this trifling detail, while I attempted not to appear too eager to hear the information she was about to impart. Eventually, she shook her head as though to clear the sticking point and continued. 'He and a friend came into The Bel ls instead. I'd only just started work there. Wasn't even meant to be on that evening but I was filling in for Maggie, who was off sick. Had terrible trouble with her chest, that one. A cold always settled on her lungs, and she'd be bedridden for weeks.' I gritted my teeth. Wished she would get to the point. 'Anyway, Amos and his friend came in. We got chatting when he came up for drinks. You know how it is. A bit later, his friend left and he stayed.

'When I said I was going to go home after my shift, he asked if he could come with me. Nothing funny like. But it was a beautiful summer night, and we sat on a bench in the park round the corner from home. I still lived with my parents back then. And we talked into the early hours about our hopes, our dreams. It got cooler, and he put his jacket around me. He was so romantic and there was this fabulous connection. Six weeks later we were married.'

'How wonderful,' Susannah cooed. She had always been a sucker for a soppy romance. 'A genuine love at first sight meeting.' After all the years it was still hard for me to believe that only hours before this fateful meeting, he had told me he would see me in church.

'It really was,' and she sent me a discreet wink as she added a giggle, 'and we still love each other as much to this day.' I bet she had been wanting to share this story with me for as long as I had wanted to hear it.

'That is nice,' I said, to fit in with the general murmurings around the table.

Evelyn looked directly at me. 'Yes, I was lucky and managed to snatch him out from under the nose of a competitor.' I fixed my smile as a sour taste developed in my mouth.

'No!' With the dropping of this additional titbit Susannah must have been in danger of falling, so close to the edge of her seat was she sitting. I had no idea what Evelyn's intentions were or what she was about to share.

'Oh yes.' Evelyn had warmed to her theme now she had an audience hanging on her every word. 'I found out later he was due to get married only two days later, but his passion for me was that powerful he knew he couldn't go through with it.'

'So, he jilted his bride and left her at the altar on their wedding day?' I could not help but chip in, suitably aghast, but rewarded by a disapproving gasp from Susannah. A split-second later Evelyn realised she was about to make her magnificent husband look like a real heel, but to give her her due, she quickly recovered.

'Oh, no, no. He could never have brought himself to do that. He made sure he visited her and her family first thing and broke off the engagement.' She placed her hand upon the table as though to emphasise the point as she continued, 'I admit it wasn't easy for him, but he faced up to it like a man.' A noise escaped me that sounded remarkably like *pfftt*. But the others believed every word. I could see it in the way they leaned in as she finished. 'The main thing is we ended up together, which is the way it should be with true love.' She placed one hand over her heart while I excused myself, unable to listen to any more of her drivel.

13. Tracking

Now

It is 49 years, 345 days since I last saw Rosie.

I now know Amos is meeting up with Agnes Peach on a Wednesday morning and Manda Babcock on a Friday afternoon. But I have yet to discover what he has been doing with his Tuesday afternoons and I am not sure how to find out without it being blindingly obvious what I am up to.

It is somewhere in the village because he walks there. And, as with the other visits, he is gone for a couple of hours. So, on this Tuesday I decide to follow him using the ruse that I am going to the shop for something. Hopefully I can narrow down which part of the village he is walking to.

I get myself ready and wait poised in my favourite seat, watching to see when he leaves. Right on cue, he walks down his path, and he is carrying a plastic bag with what appears to be a box inside.

As soon as he is a couple of hundred yards along the road, I slip out of my cottage with a shopping bag held in the crook of my arm. What I have not noticed, despite all my looking out of the window, is that it is raining. I am wearing the wrong coat and do not have an umbrella, but I dare not go back for either.

I try to behave normally but find myself creeping along as though I am furtively following someone and have to forcibly tell myself to act sensibly. Fortunately, at this time on a rainy Tuesday afternoon, there is no one around to see me.

Amos walks straight past the shop and now I am undecided on what action to take. As far as I can tell, he has been unaware of my presence to date, but I do not want him to catch me out and I cannot think of any excuse as to why I would be going further than the shop. Instead, I enter Sharon's Stores but turn immediately up the first aisle where I can keep a watch on Amos for as long as I can, out of the window. I am leaning over the shelves, craning my neck and am absorbed in why he had crossed the road when, 'What are you looking at?' close to my ear startles me. I spin round to find Sharon directly behind me.

'God, you made me jump.' My hand is on my chest as though to prevent my heart from leaping out of it.

'You're behaving oddly.' Sharon crosses her arms as though waiting for an answer.

'I was just… um, just…' I flounder around for a reasonable excuse for my behaviour. '… keeping an eye on a suspicious vehicle. Yes, that is what I was doing.' Sharon's eyes narrow and she peers past me and out of the window.

'I can't see any vehicle. What was it like?'

'Oh, you know, white van, no distinguishing features. It was travelling slowly. Like it was casing the houses.'

'I didn't see it come past.'

'You were probably busy with a customer, never mind, it has gone now.'

'I don't suppose you did anything sensible like get a number plate?'

'Sadly not, it was covered in mud,' I say, and I turn to the fresh produce to get some vegetables for dinner.

I ignore the suspicious, 'Hmmm…' Sharon ends the conversation with before she walks back towards her till. Considering she is the biggest nosy-parker and gossip in the village, I find it astonishing she is not on to Amos already. She is only too happy to mention the fact Ned has been round to see me, yet Saint Amos seems to be able to do anything and she is oblivious. I know I am going to have to get all my information together on his movements before I expose him, and I am glad I have more to add to my file now. He'd crossed the road and, even from my compromised position, I could see that he headed up the drive of the Crosses' house. There has been much speculation about them over the years, the pampas grass front and centre a dead giveaway as to where their proclivities lie, even I have heard the gossip, and I know for a fact Amos and Evelyn had never been in the Crosses' social circle. Although now, when I come to think of it, it was Evelyn who had made a point of telling me that one day, not Amos. Maybe now he was single again, he was less reticent about who he fraternised with.

14. No Patterns to See Here

Now

It is 49 years, 347 days since I last saw Rosie.

On Thursday morning, I follow two teenage girls into the shop. Both push prams. There is not a wedding ring between them and, as always when confronted with such girls, while I am happy for them, a vein of green envy runs straight through my soul. I know them from school, and they are as keen to show off their babies as I am to peek beneath the hoods. Rosy cheeks, pudgy hands, and soft curls lie across unblemished skin. Lovely.

They have no idea how lucky they are, these girls. The choices they have not had to make. Not for them the shame of unwedded motherhood. The threat of gossip that would ruin their future. They take it for granted, of course. Why wouldn't they? They have never known life to be any different, but it has taken decades for them to get to enjoy the freedoms they have.

I am all in favour of those freedoms. Evelyn was not. It was one of the many things about which she never held back on giving her views. Harping on about the irresponsible youth of today, which was rich given her husband's history. Confident in her point of view, she was one of those people who was always correct and often condescending to those who disagreed with her, talking to them as though they were a lower lifeform. She had the blousy personality to carry it off, of course. I have seen others carried along with her beliefs and as they agreed with everything she said, it was as though they had lost any ability to think for themselves.

Astonishing.

She also always knew best how everything should be done. Organising an event, she would be the one directing operations. Often, to cause a little anarchy, I would do what *I* wanted instead. I mean, does it actually matter how you fold a napkin at the village hall banquet? Apparently it does, but I did not even care when she dressed me down in front of everyone for getting it wrong. Because it was such a trivial matter. But nothing was trivial for her. Everything mattered. Everything had to be done just so.

Alice, Sally and Susannah had all at different times commented on her somewhat forceful nature and that I appeared to take the brunt of what in their eyes was bullying, but I would laugh it off as it just being the way she was.

Of course, her pity for me was such she perceived me to be some sort of pet project. For years she was intent on pairing me off with any single man she came across in the area. When her scheming did not work, and when it became possible, she did a lot of homework researching online dating. She would bore me rigid with her pronouncements of what I needed to do in order to get a man, when *I* did not need to do anything. It did not matter if I would say I was quite happy on my own, my opinion held no sway at all. It was as if she could not understand how a woman could be complete if she did not have a man. This interference of hers in my life, I suspect, grated on Amos.

You shouldn't speak ill of the dead, but life was certainly easier without her around. For me, at least.

Ned comes round in the afternoon to sort out a dripping tap I texted him about earlier in the week. Although he arrives late for lunch, I am able to give him some of my curried parsnip soup and freshly made bread as again he has not eaten. He fixes the tap in a jiffy, which allows us a lovely couple of hours under the covers before he has to rush off.

It is at moments like this, as I cuddle up to him under the duvet, that I allow myself to daydream about having a future with him. I know in all likelihood it will never become a reality but it is nice to have someone in my life who would be with me if they could.

15. Friday the 13th

It is 49 years, 348 days since I last saw Rosie.

When Sharon called earlier in the week, I was happy to agree to help out in the shop Friday afternoon because it gave me the opportunity to see if Amos visits Manda Babcock again. I am there by twelve, as Sharon wants to get to the Cash-and-Carry. I deal with all the customers quickly and efficiently to keep them moving along, allowing me as much time as possible to watch Manda's bungalow.

Shortly after two o'clock, I see Amos walk along the pavement on the opposite side of the road. He has something under his arm. A book, perhaps? He lets himself into Manda's home.

I carry on serving the steady trickle of customers, although I am distracted by what is going on over the road, so I do not hear the first time Kyle Croxton speaks.

'I am sorry. What did you say?' I scan the chocolates and flowers in his basket.

'I said I was sorry to hear about Ned.' He uses his phone to pay.

'What about Ned?' He stares at me. Gulps.

'I thought you'd have heard. Sorry, never mind.' He grabs his shopping as if about to make a quick getaway.

'Heard what? You can't leave it there. What about him?' His face falls at me putting him on the spot, but he does stay put and tries to meet my gaze.

'Um...' he swallows, his Adam's apple bobbing in his throat, 'Erm, I'm sorry to be the one to tell you but, er, he, um, passed away this morning.' The floor beneath my feet sways and breath leaves my lungs as I grab the edge of the counter to steady myself. Kyle's brow creases. 'Are you okay?' I wave away his concern.

'That can't be right. I only saw him yesterday.' He must be mistaken. Must be. People do not just die. I catch myself. Of course they do. My dad did.

'I'm sorry, I thought you'd have heard. I popped into the pub to book a table and it was all anyone was talking about.'

'What did you hear, exactly?'

'Only that he died this morning.'

'And you are sure it was Ned, our Ned, they were talking about?'

'Yes, he's done some decorating for us, I knew who they meant. I thought you'd have known already, or I wouldn't have said anything.'

'Why would you think I would have known already?' Alert to what he is insinuating, I need to know what he knows.

'Well, I, er, thought you were close.' *Uh oh.* I struggle to swallow round the hard lump gathered in my throat.

'Close? We were not close. I knew him, that is all. He did work for me, like he did for many people.' Thinking quickly, I feel disloyal at denying our true relationship, but I have to, to preserve his memory and protect his family.

'Sorry. I must have the wrong end of the stick.'

'Yes, you must have, but I am sorry for snapping. It was the shock. Thank you for telling me.' He nods but remains crestfallen. I try to pick him up, indicating towards the flowers and chocolates. 'I hope Olivia spoils you as much.' He smiles, mumbles his thanks and leaves the shop, no doubt relieved to get away from the awkward situation.

As soon as the door closes behind him, I sit heavily on the stool, collapsing as though my legs have lost the ability to keep me upright any longer. It took all the strength I had to remain standing and bat away Kyle's insinuations. I hope I played it cool enough, for I would hate anything to get out now after Ned and I have kept our relationship hidden for this long. His wife maybe beyond caring, but it would still be awful for the rest of his family to find out he was having an affair. I shudder at the thought of being discovered as the other woman.

Tears prick the backs of my eyes and I take a tissue from my pocket to wipe away those that overflow, then blow my nose. Fortunately, the shop is empty, and I have a few moments to collect myself. I am reeling. Ned has died? How can that have happened? I know it is not the same, as we had only been together for a few years, but I still loved him and I realised something of what my mum must have experienced on hearing the news about Dad. Poor woman. I do not think I appreciated her pain at the time.

I am anxious to go home so I can have some privacy and I wonder when Sharon will be back. I dread someone else coming in and wanting to talk about it. How will I manage to hide my emotions again? I glance out of the window to see if there is any sign of her. There isn't, but I see Amos walking back along the pavement. Just over two hours have passed since he entered Manda's property.

Fortunately, there are only a couple more customers before I see Sharon's truck pull in, and neither mention Ned. Usually, I would give her some time to unload or a hand if I can, particularly as she is unwell, but as soon as the shop is empty, I pop my head into the stockroom.

'Sorry, Sharon, but I have to go home. I have got a splitting headache and need to lie down.'

'That's not really convenient, Dora. I've got all this to sort out.'

'Then call another volunteer. Amos is around. I have just seen him. Call him. I need to go.'

'Okay, okay. If you have to.' She makes no effort to hide the irritation in her voice as she puts the box she is carrying with some difficulty on the floor and follows me back through to the shop. I can hear her grumbling under her breath, but I don't care. I reach behind the counter for my bag and leave without uttering another word, and, I note again, without a thank you from Sharon either.

I walk swiftly, brushing away the tears that fall as I pray I see no one I know. As I close the front door behind me, my breath judders out with relief and, not making it further than the bottom step of the stairs, my emotions release and the tears flow freely. Tissues quickly become sodden and I use my sleeve to wipe at my face. Eventually my tears are spent, and getting fresh tissues from the kitchen I dry my eyes and blow my nose. My head pounds with a headache from the tension.

I am not sure what to do.

Struggling to believe what has happened I do not want to appear to be overly interested by asking anyone about it. I draw the curtains, all of them, even those in the bay window, and shut myself off from the outside world. No one can see me in here.

I pour myself a glass of wine and deliberate on whether I should call him or not. It is not what we do, call. When I have something for him to do, I send him a text message and he will reply within a day to let me know when he will be round.

'That is probably the best thing to do,' I say out loud, and reach for my phone. This is how I can find out the truth. I send the text, drain my glass and refill it. He will reply, I know he will, and the news Kyle told me will have been a huge misunderstanding. It must be. Sharon had not heard about it and she hears everything first. I try to find this reassuring, but I cannot settle and spend some time tidying to keep myself occupied. I contemplate dinner but cannot face eating, so leave it.

I finish the bottle and put the television on. I watch the local news, but there is nothing on there about Ned dying. Although why would there be unless it had happened in some newsworthy way? I check the local newspaper sites on my iPad but again there is nothing. Of course, I don't know what happened, or how, or in fact where he supposedly died, therefore I have no clues to go on. In hindsight, I should have asked Kyle more questions, but I panicked. Stupid of me. Ned and I being involved was probably the last thing on Kyle's mind, and I blew it all out of proportion.

I keep checking my phone, even though it would be highly unusual for Ned to respond this quickly.

I am not a big drinker. But at times of stress or high emotion I find a glass or two helps relax me. Tonight, I am tempted to open a second bottle but eventually decide not to. Thinking sensibly, I have to go round to Alice's for coffee and cake in the morning and do not want to be the worse for wear. But the wine I have consumed has done nothing to calm my frayed nerves and, unable to concentrate on the television because my eyes continually flick back to my phone, I decide to have an early night.

My book is no better at focusing my mind and I turn several pages without taking in a word. Eventually I switch off the light and lie in the darkness, unable to quieten my frenetic thoughts which spring from one scenario to another.

I watch the hours pass. My phone ridiculously clamped in my hand when I know he is never going to reply during the night.

At some point after five, I nod off, but I am awake again by seven.

There has been no response to my text.

It is 49 years, 349 days since I last saw Rosie.

I consider cancelling coffee and cake by pleading some sort of illness, but Alice is bound to come over to check on me if I do. Besides, I need to keep up appearances. So, despite feeling shocking, I make cake. It is a tray bake, mixed spice and sultanas liven it up and I put a couple of slices on a plate to take round, the rest in the freezer for next week's coffee morning.

I get my chores done quickly, keen to keep busy, and the cottage is spick and span by the time I am due to meet Alice. She opens the door as though she was standing on the other side waiting for my knock.

'Oh, Dora, I'm sorry. You must be devastated.'

'About what?'

'Well about Ned, of course.' Her hand comes to her mouth. 'Oh, God, you have heard the news?' It is true then. My hand in my pocket releases my phone from its grasp. Despite hanging on to this last fragile tendril of hope, I now know I will not be receiving a reply to my text and my heart sinks. I swallow to clear the thickness in my throat.

'Yes, I have heard, terribly sad, although devastated might be a bit strong. He did just do odd jobs for me.' My heart twists in protest at the guilt I feel as I distance myself from my lover. Alice turns from the counter where she is making coffee. Her brow furrowed.

'Oh. I thought you and he had something going on. He appeared to come round most weeks.' I am surprised she knows this, considering she is out at work during the day, but also alarmed she thinks it. I am reminded of the comment Kyle made yesterday. Alice places the coffee on the table and takes her seat.

'Not every week.'

'You look tired.' Which is what every woman wants to hear.

'I didn't sleep well.' I hope that might deflect her from her opening topic of the morning, but it does not.

'Thursdays, wasn't it? I only noticed because it's the day I have to spend the afternoon on one of our sites and I come right past here.'

Of course you do.

'I liked him to keep on top of all the small jobs I have. Stops them building up. I would send him a text with what needed doing and he would fit me in the next time he was free.'

Was it always Thursdays?

Alice takes a bite of the cake. I cannot face eating my piece even though I missed breakfast, but I sip at the coffee to show willing.

'Anyway, you're lucky it didn't happen the day before when he was at yours.'

'I am lucky what didn't happen? I don't know how he, er, died.' Struggling to get the word out, I cough as though to clear my throat.

'Heart attack, apparently. The men in the workshop were talking about it. He was working for some lady and collapsed.'

'Poor Ned.' My heart bled for him. He had had a miserable few years struggling to carry on working and bring in the money needed to look after his wife, and now he was gone. Much too young too. His poor wife. How was she going to cope? Although I suppose seeing as how she did not actually recognise him anymore, she would probably not realise he was no longer there. This thought only makes me sadder.

Thankfully, Alice soon moves off onto other news. Mostly things to do with the dreadful time she is having at work, and I can get away with half listening, because I have heard it all before.

As I partially concentrate, and try to put Ned out of my mind for this short time, I think about the fact Alice is fifty. Since finding out her age a few years ago it is impossible to be in her company and not think of Rosie. I look at Alice's life and wonder what Rosie has done with hers. Most importantly, I hope she is not as miserable about her circumstances as Alice is. Or at least if she is, she has gumption enough to do something about it. But I also question the bigger things. Did she marry? Did she have children? Could I be a grandmother? Does she work? If she does, what at? What are her interests? Where does she live? The questions that roll around my head are endless. Since giving up work and with more time on my hands, when I particularly want to torture myself, like now, I imagine Rosie's life and all I have missed out on.

I have never told a soul about her or Amos. Anyone who knew, my mum and dad, Cara and Tom, are all either gone or at such a distance for it not to matter.

Although that is not entirely true. There was one other person who knew about Rosie, albeit briefly. Evelyn. But she is no longer around, either.

16: The One Constant. Then. Now. Forever.

I only ever wear one piece of jewellery. A silver locket. There is a curl of dark hair inside. Rosie's. The constant in my everyday thoughts. While I have missed out on my own little girl's life, I have watched Amos and Evelyn's girls grow up and tried not to be resentful. Over the years I have always imagined Rosie as part of the family, the oldest of the three sisters.

Once settled in Melton, I left my new address and telephone number with the adoption agency. They have a file about me and Rosie. Before Rosie was born, I bought two identical small teddy bears. One I left with her at the hospital, the other is in our file. My hope is that should she ever come looking for me she will recognise the bear and know she was loved. I have spent every day since she would have become an adult waiting for the phone to ring. But there are some days I pin my hopes on her calling more than others. Specifically, Christmas Day, birthdays and especially Mother's Day.

Each day when I wake, the first thing I do is say how long it is since I last saw Rosie. Today it is 49 years, 350 days.

Each year on Rosie's birthday, I celebrate quietly and alone by writing her a letter. I have a large shoebox full of them now. There is also a note in there to explain who I am writing to should I die and someone else finds the letters. My hope is that they will get them to her somehow.

I have rather fancifully imagined the call will come on Mother's Day this year. This is because it falls on the twenty-ninth of March, which is also Rosie's birthday. Rosie's fiftieth birthday. If she does not call then, when will she?

That day, marked on my calendar, is only two weeks from today. When I think of it, of the possibility of her calling on that day, my stomach turns over nervously. How would the conversation go?

I cannot bear the thought Rosie may hate me for what I did. Might not have had the perfect life I had imagined for her. What if she rings and her words are full of loathing?

I am consumed by my memories of her. By thoughts of my little girl being out in the big wide world without her mum. Although, she is no longer a little girl. And, she had a mother and a father.

I am sure her adoptive parents will have done an excellent job of bringing her up. I have to think this, I cannot bear considering any alternative. But I wonder all the time. I wonder if they kept her name. I wonder what her interests are, what she excels in, for there must be something. Everyone excels at something. Even if it is mundane stuff like filing and accounts. Most of all I wonder what she looks like, if I would be able to see myself or Amos in her features. Also, while I know I left her in Scotland and most likely she is still there, it has never stopped me from examining the faces of every girl or woman of her age I pass in the street. Wondering, what if? What if? I also wonder when she found out about the adoption. How she took the news. How it has affected her, if at all? Mostly, I wonder if she is happy and content with her life.

Part of me, a tiny part I do not like, somewhat selfishly hopes there is a small piece of her that feels incomplete, that feels like it is missing something. That it is missing me. Has she ever wondered where she came from? What she might find if she sought me out?

Have those thoughts put her off making contact?

I long for her call. I always have done. Every day. I have made sure my details are correct with the relevant agencies. I check in with them once a year in case there have been any enquiries. Once they became a thing, I made sure I had a mobile. I make certain it is always charged and with me, but you cannot rely on the signal around here. So, I keep the landline. Besides, I am of an age where I turn to the landline first.

Of course, I have faced the reality of the situation and fully appreciate the huge loyalty I am sure she feels to her adoptive parents. I try to be fair and generous to them, but calling them her mum and dad is, for me, a step too far. I have tried it but the flash of jealousy conjured inside my heart is too much. It taints my thoughts for the rest of the day. Despite this, I fully expect her to be loyal to them – they will have brought her up to be so, quite rightly. But on this I am torn because although I want her to have had fabulous parents who gave her a wonderful life, it does not serve my purpose for them to have been too fantastic because I expect it means she will make no attempt to contact me until they have died. Therefore, I suspect this is a game of survival. Of who will outlive the other…

17: Fretting

It is 49 years, 351 days since I last saw Rosie.

Since the news about Ned, three days ago, I cannot settle, or sleep. I take brief naps on the underused sofa when I feel tired, but jerk awake half an hour later. My appetite has gone too, my waistband already looser than it was. I suppose it is all part of the grieving process, although I do not remember being like this with my parents. I was not this desperate, this inconsolable. Maybe the difference is I have lost a lover. When my dad died, I was caught up in looking after Mum which helped me through the worst days. Then, when Mum went, I had a lot of support despite having no family left. Mum's friends and the community I had grown up in rallied round and I had plenty of kind ears willing to listen. Now, I have no one I can talk to. No one to confide in.

For the first time in fifty years, I have someone other than Rosie occupying my mind.

I miss him. Despite only seeing him at most once a week, I miss the reassuring presence of him being around. Sometimes I would glimpse his van disappearing off up the road, or round a corner, and it would put a bounce in my step all day, a smile on my face. Now I spend hours reliving every moment of the time he refitted my kitchen. Those two glorious weeks when he was in my cottage every day, all day, and we had chatted and laughed together as though we were a proper couple. I had thought that one day, maybe, all our days would be like this. Together.

I ponder the lunches we shared before he tackled my list of jobs. The things we discussed, the way he put me at ease. Our time in bed together. The likelihood of me ever having sex with anyone ever again.

I fret about his last moments. About him being in pain or scared. I hate the thought he knew he was dying and was alone. Alice said I was lucky he did not have his heart attack when he was at mine, but at least I would have comforted him. Or even saved him. What if this other client didn't do CPR on him? I know how to do it, but plenty do not. What if she didn't even try and left him to die?

As I sit in my chair and stare out at the world, I feel anger boil up from deep down inside. I need to move to burn off the energy I feel running through my veins, but do not want to bump into anyone I know by walking round the village. My supplies are also running low but I can't face going to Sharon's Stores. Much as I love living in a village, I am not keen on everyone knowing what I have bought for my dinner or judging me on the number of chocolate bars I have in my basket. I feel guilty for not always supporting Sharon but since turning vegetarian some five years ago I have struggled to get all my shopping there as, understandably, she does not carry as large a range of vegetables or vegetarian options as I would like and this is how I justify my occasional trips to the supermarket. I also like their anonymity.

A couple of hours later, I hear the reassuring clink of glass against glass precede me as I push my well-stocked trolley across the car park to load up my car. Mission accomplished.

Once back home, I unpack everything and put it away. I look at the food I have bought but none of it appeals to me, so despite it only being early evening, I reward myself for a job well done by opening a bottle of wine.

I wonder when we will hear the date for the funeral, and if I should go to it. Is it going to look odd if I go, or worse if I do not? All these thoughts and a thousand more tumble around my brain throughout the evening and although I refill my glass in the hope of dulling the noise, I still do not sleep.

18: The Unravelling

Tuesday – it is 49 years, 352 days since I last saw Rosie.

I heard this morning. The funeral is a week on Friday, at a crematorium near where he lived, some twenty miles from here. I have until then to decide whether I go or not.

Between now and then, I am going to busy myself by keeping my eye on Amos and getting my notes together about his activities so I can take my concerns to the police. I spend the morning sitting at my table in the window collating the information I have already. Using my skills from a lifetime in admin, I set out his timetable, colour-coded, of course.

I write up what I know about his victims and create files for each of them which I can add information to. As I put this all together, I become uncertain whether perhaps I should take some direct action now rather than doing the paperwork. I sit back and consider what I have and reassure myself I am doing the right thing. Everyone sees Amos as a paragon of virtue around here, therefore I must have the evidence in black and white. The police will never believe me if I turn up with only vague details of his suspicious behaviour.

I decide I need to follow Amos' movements until the funeral, by which time I will have several weeks of indisputable evidence to show them. With it being Tuesday today and nearly lunchtime, I need to make a move. I skip lunch and as the forecast is for intermittent icy showers, I wrap up warmly and add my waterproof coat and hat, which I jam onto my head. Between hat and scarf there is little of my face on show.

I am getting ahead of Amos this week. I believe I know where he will be going this afternoon, so I want to position myself to get the proof.

Jeremy and Petula Cross own an imposing property which is set well back from the road, up an incline and has plenty of space around it. Opposite are some smaller properties and between two of these there is a public footpath. It is narrow as it passes between the six-foot-high walls that border each property. Walls which are covered in rambling plants. They might not be particularly abundant in March but are enough to shield an onlooker for a short while before raising any suspicions.

If I am spotted in the area, anyone will assume I am off for a walk. The villagers are accustomed to seeing me tramping all around the local area, so they will not see this as unusual. And if I am seen loitering, for want of a better word, I will say I am sending a text. My mobile phone is in my pocket, ready to be waved as evidence.

I ensure I have all I need and I am in position by ten to two, ending up using the high walls as shelter from a shower, which was indeed icy. As it recedes to little more than the occasional spot or two, the sun comes out and, as always, I never fail to be astonished at how fickle our weather can be. The sky is now a perfect blue.

Amos arrives within a minute or two of the church bell chiming the hour. The front of his trousers is darker than the back where he got caught in the shower, and the thought of his discomfort makes me smile.

I remove my camera from my pocket and take a few shots of him arriving, walking up the drive and knocking on the door.

He carries a bag again which I can clearly see contains a box, but I cannot make out what it is.

Petula Cross welcomes him inside and I walk home, calling into the shop on my way. Sharon is busy serving, but once those customers have gone, the shop is empty bar us two. I am not sure why I have come in but now I am here I feel I should buy something. I wander the aisles seeking inspiration, and finding little, choose some packets of crisps and a bottle of wine.

'When I got back on Friday, you didn't tell me Ned had died.' Sharon's accusatory tone puts my back up as I put my basket down next to the till for her.

'I didn't know then.'

'That wasn't why you had to leave?'

'No, I told you, I had a headache.' She does a poor job of covering the fact she is rolling her eyes.

'Well, just so you know, I don't appreciate being one of the last to hear. The village shop is meant to be a hive of local knowledge and information for people.'

'I am sure you have more than made up for it since.'

'What's that supposed to mean?'

'It means I am sure you have picked over all the fine details and spread the gossip far and wide.'

'Information, not gossip. You know I'm not one of those.' It is my turn to roll my eyes and I do not even care if she is annoyed, although if she is she covers it well, because…

'Actually,' and she smiles for the first time, 'I don't suppose you're available to do Friday afternoon, are you? I've got a follow-up with the doctor.'

… she needs me.

As it happens, it suits my purposes, so I agree to work from lunchtime on Friday and I do not even make her beg.

Once back home, I open the bottle rather than boil the kettle and I settle down to wait for Amos to return. I take a couple more photos for the sake of completeness when he does, and set about updating my notes with the day's surveillance report.

Wednesday – It is 49 years, 353 days since I last saw Rosie.

It is the coffee morning at the village hall and, if Amos sticks to his previous pattern, he will miss it because he will be with Agnes Peach. Again, I want evidence and while obtaining it will be trickier, as there is nowhere for me to hide, I have come up with a cunning plan. I have not actually practised it, because there is the chance Amos will see me, but what I aim to do is wait in my bedroom until I see him leave his cottage. Once he is walking away up the road, I will open the window wide. I should be able to take some photos of him entering Agnes' front garden and, because of the curve of the road, knocking on her door.

I am anxious about this not working and having to wait another week, therefore I get into position early. I check the catch on the window will open when required and fiddle with the camera, checking and rechecking it is ready. Fortunately, it is a still, dry day, so there should be no issues, as long as Amos does not spot me.

The minutes passed slowly as I wait for him to make an appearance, but eventually he leaves his place, still using his stick, and crosses the road. As soon as his back is to me, I ease aside the catch and slowly open the window to its full extent.

I had pulled a chair up under the window earlier. I now climb onto it carefully, and then take a sneaky peek to make sure he is not looking in this direction, and no one else is around. Once I am happy, I lean out as far as feels safe and start snapping away. I do this both through the glass of the window and by holding the camera under the window frame, hoping it is pointing in roughly the right direction. The main thing is to make no quick moves, particularly as he turns to go through Agnes's gate and walks up her pathway. I do not want to draw attention to myself.

Once the door has closed behind Amos, I climb down off my chair and shut the window. Sitting on the edge of my bed I have a quick scan through the photos and although I have to delete several blurred efforts, I am happy with what I have got.

I have been so preoccupied with getting this part of my day right I realise I forgot to take the rest of the tray bake out of the freezer earlier. There is no time to defrost it now as I have got to get to the coffee morning. I put my coat on, place the camera in its pocket and retrieve the frozen cake before I leave the house. I will have to give it a quick blitz in the microwave once I am at the village hall.

Susannah Bugby and Sally Button are already there along with several other villagers, and while Sally is chatting to a couple at the other end of the hall, there is a look of relief on Susannah's face when I walk in.

'Ah, there you are. I was getting worried about you.'

'No need to, Susannah. I am running a bit late, that is all.'

'Thanks for the cake. I've put a plate out.'

'I need to defrost it first.' Susannah's brow creases as she stares at me.

'That's unlike you. You're usually so organised. Are you sure everything's okay?'

'Perfectly, thank you,' I say, and I hit the button on the microwave, my tray bake slices turning inside.

I set about organising the kitchen as I always do and I leave Susannah and Sally to face the public. It is a busy morning, and I am happy providing plenty of boiling water for tea and manning the coffee machine where necessary. The pile of crockery builds next to the sink, but I soon get on top of it.

'Why don't you come and have a coffee, Dora?' Susannah calls through the hatch.

'I've already had one,' I lie.

'Come and have a chat then?'

'I can't today. I've got to get back.'

'Another delivery?' I sense the tone in Susannah's voice.

'No, just something I need to do.' I take a tea towel and start drying and putting away the cups and plates.

'You're retired now, Dora. It's alright to allow yourself some time off, you know. You're running round as busy as you were when you were working. Anyway, I wanted to see how you are after the news about Ned. Bit of a shock, wasn't it?'

'Yes, of course it was, but I'm fine.'

'It's such a shame because he was a lovable old rogue. I'll miss him.' I place the mug in my hand in the cupboard and catch her eye.

'He will be a sad loss to the entire village.' She sighs and turns away as if she is disappointed in my answers, but I do not want to get into this conversation. I do not want to give myself away by sharing feelings. I do not want her to know my already damaged heart is breaking once more. Or tell her I dreamt about him last night and woke up with tears streaming down my face. What I want to do is leave, go home and have a glass of wine. Because coffee is doing nothing to numb the pain.

I am on my way home soon after. As I turn the corner into Main Street, I have my camera ready to go in case, like before,

I am in the right place at the right time to see Amos leaving Agnes's cottage. This time though, there is no sign of him and with no idea if he has already left or not, there is little point in me hanging around. Besides, there is the last glass in a bottle waiting for me.

Once home, I am surprised to find no unfinished bottle. I must have been mistaken, so reach for another from the box under the stairs. I am soon settled at my table in the window writing up my journal while I keep a lookout for any movement over the road.

It is another half an hour before I see Amos strolling back. While it is annoying not to have the photographic proof of him leaving Agnes, I take a few shots now through the net curtain and make a note of the time for my records.

Thursday – It is 49 years, 354 days since I last saw Rosie.

After yet another night of less than three hours' sleep, I am awake by five, tearful and exhausted. My brain is wired with all the things it thinks I have to do, when in fact there is little to occupy me today. I am unable to nod back off. I take a couple of painkillers for my throbbing head, make an early cup of tea and sit in the darkness until the sun rises a little after six.

I think I can eat breakfast this morning, for the first time this week. I make toast and a pot of tea, but when it comes to it, my appetite is so diminished, I barely manage half a piece before I am full.

I rarely watch the television but put it on this morning to catch up on the news. Unusually, I leave it on as the daytime programmes begin, wanting the company and distraction.

There is a rattle of the letterbox mid-morning. I think it is the post, but when I go to check the mat, I find a circular advertising *The Poison Pen*, the Murder Mystery only a week on Saturday. I smile because it gives me an idea for another way to keep myself busy.

Years ago, I used to take any opportunity offered to assist in one of the classrooms. While parental help was often hard to come by, I enjoyed stepping in and spending time with all the year groups, although the younger classes were my favourites. My input was most often needed for craft activities when there would be around thirty children busy sewing with blunted needles that constantly needed rethreading, painting, when much of the paint never made it onto the paper, or cutting and sticking when child-friendly scissors were wielded and there could never be enough eyes in the room to ensure no accidents.

I find the most recent village newsletter which covers several parishes and give myself up to my own crafting morning. Later, after the job is complete, I remove my latex gloves and bury them deep in my rubbish bin. It is collection day tomorrow; my timing could not be better.

I prefer the bottles with the screw tops nowadays and enjoy hearing the seal break on the first twist. I have kept busier than I expected today, and toast to my success as I settle down to watch a film in the afternoon as a treat.

Friday – It is 49 years, 355 days since I last saw Rosie.

I do not enjoy working afternoons. With one eye on the clock, I never make good use of the morning, knowing I have got to be somewhere by a certain time. This is how it is on Friday morning when I know I have to be at Sharon's Stores shortly after lunch. I cannot settle to anything. I am also agitated because I want to capture Amos entering Manda's bungalow. Therefore, I have a liquid lunch and get to the shop early.

'You're keen. I wasn't expecting you for another half hour at least.'

'I thought I would get here in good time, so you are not rushing for your appointment.'

'Very thoughtful.' Sharon manages to say this in a way that makes it feel like it is not thoughtful at all. I lean down beside her to put my bag out of sight under the counter. When I stand again, she frowns at me. 'Have you just come from the pub?'

'Of course not. What a thing to say,' and without waiting for her response I turn to straighten the display in the fruit and veg chiller cabinet, from where I can also keep watch on Manda's place. As I feel Sharon's keen eye on me, a flush spreads up my cheeks.

There is no one in the shop when she calls out, 'I'm going out back to get ready.' I raise my hand in response but carry on being busy. But as soon as she is out of sight, I nip round to the confectionery section, choose a packet of extra strong mints and pop a couple in my mouth.

She is back a few minutes later, by which time I am behind the till as a couple of customers have come in. She shows no subtlety at all in getting as close to me as possible and I hear the sharp inhale through those pinched nostrils of hers. I sense her disappointment as she contemplates her findings and, as she puts on her jacket, she tells me she is leaving.

I am relieved when she has gone and I can get on with my primary task of the day. Digging my camera out of my bag, I make sure it is ready. I keep everything crossed that the shop is empty when Amos appears. Straight after lunchtime is usually a quiet period, so I should be lucky.

I stay behind the till as I can see straight out of the door and across the road. I rush through the couple of customers that do come in then as soon as Amos comes into view, I hop off the stool and scurry over to the door to get a better view. His hand is in his pocket and I bet he is searching for Manda's key. I take a couple of shots, then more as he approaches Manda's front door. I am delighted when there is a clear one of him using a key to gain access.

'What are you doing?' makes me jump out of my skin. I lower the camera and Sally Button is at my side, peering to see whatever it was I was taking photos of. Thankfully, Amos is no longer in view.

'A Draft Warbler,' I say, my words coming out in a hurry. 'At a guess; I was trying to get a photo.'

'A Draft Warbler? Do you mean Dartford Warbler?' I nod enthusiastically, somewhat amazed I had come up with a name even close to that of an actual bird. 'It's not likely, is it? Not around here. And certainly not as early in the year as this.'

'Oh, that is disappointing. I was sure that is what it was.' Sally's eyes narrow as she studies me.

'I didn't know you were into birding?' *And I didn't know you were.*

'I am only an amateur. You are right, I was probably mistaken.'

'Let's have a look, I can soon tell you.' She reaches for my camera, and I move it swiftly away.

'Not necessary.' My laugh sounds forced as I brush off her offer and walk away to return to the safe space behind the counter. 'I didn't manage to get a photo because it had flown away before I got it in focus.'

'What a shame. A sighting of a Dartford Warbler would have caused quite a stir among the twitchers. They'd have been flocking here in their droves, pun intended,' and she laughs lightly as she picks up a basket and sets off to do her shopping. I lower myself onto the stool with some relief. After that lucky escape I put my camera back into my bag and decide not to gather any further evidence. What I have got already will have to do.

I catch Sally looking at me occasionally as she wanders round the shop, and I try to appear calm when I feel anything but.

Eventually she gets to the till. As I scan the contents of her basket, I ignore the eyes I feel boring into me.

'Are you okay, Dora?'

'Yes, perfectly, thank you.'

'You don't seem quite yourself.'

'I'm tired, that's all. I'm not sleeping.'

'Oh, it's awful when you don't get enough sleep, isn't it? I go through bouts of insomnia, and it gets you down.' I nod sympathetically. 'Do you know what's causing it?'

I can hardly tell her the truth, so mutter some nonsense about not being able to switch off. From what exactly she does not question, fortunately, as I am hardly as busy as I was when I was working.

'Not long now until the Murder Mystery. That's always a good evening to look forward to.' She says this like she is trying to perk me up, but all I manage to give her in response is a brief nod. I am therefore pleased when she picks up her bag, and breathe a sigh of relief when she exits the shop.

Having got what I came for by way of photos of Amos, I cannot wait to leave and, as if it will make Sharon get back quicker, I rush all the customers through the till. In between serving people, I fret about my conversation with Sally and Sharon's earlier accusation. I need to get home where I do not have people poking their noses in my business. It is like being in a goldfish bowl in here and I do not care for it. More than once this afternoon I had the distinct impression people were prying.

'You took your time,' is how I greet Sharon on her return. I know I am being short with her, but I am anxious to leave as quickly as possible. I do at least manage to ask her how it went and if there was any diagnosis of her condition, yet. I have noticed she's started walking with a stick and the shakes in her hands are clearly visible. So, much as I am impatient to get off, I feel I should at least try to be kind.

'They're no further forward as far as I can see. I've got more tests when I get to the top of the waiting list, and who knows when that could be?' I smile sympathetically as I reach for my bag and pull my coat on, hoping she gets the point and I can slip away. 'Anything I need to know?'

'No, everything has been fine. A steady trickle of customers, no troublemakers.'

'Okay, well, I guess that's me here for the next few hours then.' She is so forlorn I cannot help but feel a pang of sympathy for her with the state she is in.

'You should close earlier. People would soon get used to it.'

'I'm not sure the shop would survive if I did. People use it because it's open long hours.'

For the first time since knowing Sharon, and I have known her since primary school, I sense a chink in her armour. She was

130

a child with more attitude than was probably good for her then, but now her confidence is at a low ebb. For a moment I consider staying, just to check she is okay, but she has caught me out like this before. Offer, and she will take. Because while I have in mind lending a hand in the shop alongside her, I know she will leave me to it and disappear into the house to make the most of her time off. And I am not in the mood to be used right now.

As I leave the shop, I know there is one thing I can rely on: Sharon will remain true to form. Not one word of thanks.

I rush home and close my front door behind me with relief, keen to be away from prying eyes and nosy questions designed to look sympathetic.

I have eaten the packet of mints through the afternoon and do not feel hungry. I toy with the idea of making a cup of tea but the milk in the fridge has gone off so I open a bottle of red instead, like many do on a Friday evening to celebrate the fact it is the weekend.

I write up my notes on Amos' trip to Manda's today while it is still daylight and I have enough light to see by. I keep half an eye on Amos' opposite and see his lights come on just as I have done over the decades.

Once I have updated my records, I refill my glass and sit back, letting my thoughts wander. As so often, they drift to the past and to a moment that I return to regularly. When Evelyn died, many things in my life changed. One of these was that I stopped going to yoga. She liked all that stuff, whereas I prefer walking in the countryside, or aerobics in the privacy of my home. The downside is that I do not think I have taken a deep breath since her death. I try now, knowing I am holding tension throughout my body, but it's impossible. My lungs are

131

incapable of filling to their full capacity before the air rushes out prematurely. I do not try again.

Instead, I down my wine and contemplate the information I have put together. I am happy I have got enough to prove to the police that Amos is up to something sinister. Patterns have formed over the last few weeks which I am sure will make them pay attention and investigate further. I still have to sort the photos, but that will be a job for next week.

At some point I fall asleep in my chair, jolting awake later, a crick in my neck. It is not yet midnight when I go to bed but I do not manage to get back to sleep.

Saturday – It is 49 years, 356 days since I last saw Rosie.

My head aches and I try not to rub at my eyes which feel gritty as I sit back in my chair the following morning. It is too much bother to go to the shop to get milk, so I drink my tea black. I make myself a piece of toast and manage half before my parched throat feels like it is closing up.

I remember it is coffee and cake day at the exact moment I hear Alice's knock on the back door. A quick glance round the kitchen tells me not to let her in, and I briefly consider pretending I am not here. But her second more insistent knock confirms she will not go away. She will jump to the conclusion I have fallen or am otherwise incapacitated, and then she will dig out the key she holds for emergencies.

I am not yet dressed, so open the door just wide enough to let my face show.

'Morning, Alice.' My voice is croaky.

'Morning.' She goes to take a step closer, then seeing I am not about to budge studies me. 'Are you okay?'

'Yes, but I overslept. I forgot what day it was. This is what happens when you retire,' I try to joke, but it is so unlike me it falls flat. 'Look, could we do this at your place this week? I have no milk.' Her eyes narrow further and I can see how perplexing she finds my behaviour. I am probably the most organised person she knows. Therefore the thought of me not having milk is indeed odd. I am going to have to do better.

But of course, she says, 'Yes, come over to mine when you're ready.' I close the door gratefully and go to take a shower.

Twenty minutes later and I am at her door, albeit without cake and smoothing my hair with my palms. I should have washed it, but did not want to hold her up any longer than I had to.

'Come in,' Alice calls, and I walk into her spotless kitchen filled with the aroma of coffee. I feel I am under inspection as she ushers me into a chair. 'It's unlike you to sleep in. Are you alright?'

I try to brush her concerns away. 'I'm fine. I did not sleep well last night, then fell asleep when I would usually be getting up...' A look of understanding passes across her face as she finishes my sentence for me, nodding as she does.

'... which is why you overslept. I see. And how do you feel now? I've done that before and it leaves you groggy, doesn't it?' It is easier to agree with her, so I do. 'The good thing is,' she continues as she carries the mugs of coffee across to the table, 'that after a bad one, you tend to sleep like a log the next night. That's what I find, anyway.' I do not want to disappoint her, but I think that is unlikely. This has been going on for a while now. I cannot remember when I last managed more than a couple of hours' sleep. Probably the night before Ned died.

133

Now I think about it. While I am physically tired, my brain will not switch off and far from groggy, it is wired. Jumpy as I am, the overload to my nervous system makes my muscles twitch, and while I try not to show it, my fingers are unable to keep still under the table.

'Have some cake,' she says, and cuts me a slice of her delicious tea bread before buttering it and pushing the small plate towards me. Usually, I love it. Now, the thought alone turns my stomach, which I do not understand as I have not yet eaten. But I am suspicious. Maybe this is a test. She has set me this task to see if I really am alright and if I fail, she will be telling everyone there is something wrong with me.

'Lovely, you know how much I love your tea bread.' I clasp my hands together under the table, threading the fingers before tightening and loosening my grip repeatedly in an attempt to still the tremors I am sure she will spot. Once this action has calmed them sufficiently, I reach for my mug of coffee, only trusting two hands to get it to my mouth safely.

'Delicious,' I announce as I place the mug carefully back on the table. Alice has a proper coffee-making machine. Nothing fancy but a step up on my instant brews. I break my tea bread in half and proceed to eat it, slowly, as I feel Alice's observant eye on me. 'How has your week been? Busy preparing for *The Poison Pen*, I expect.' I wash the tea bread down with a sip of coffee and take another mouthful.

'Yes, although there's not much line-learning like with a play, and we all carry props with reminders on them, so we remember to pass on the relevant clues. It's more about staying in character, which isn't that easy when you're mingling among an audience filled with friends rather than being on a stage.

Actually, that reminds me, do you mind if we pass on coffee and cake next Saturday as we're having a final run through?'

I nod my agreement, having committed the last piece of tea bread to my mouth where it cloys, sticking to the roof, and I reach for my mug, needing liquid to swallow. It will be good to give it a miss as I will be recovering from Ned's funeral and trying to build myself up to go to the Murder Mystery.

'And how about you, Dora? How's your week been?' I am under scrutiny as she gazes at me and I cannot meet her eye.

'It has been okay. I have kept busy. Helped out at the shop yesterday.'

'Are you going to Ned's funeral?'

'Possibly. Probably. How about you?'

'No, I'll be at work. I wasn't as close to him as you.'

'I was not close to him.'

'You say that, but his death seems to have affected you quite badly.' I shrug. 'You're not sleeping. You're barely eating—'

'I have just eaten your cake.'

'It's plain to see you're losing weight, Dora. I'm not sure you're looking after yourself.' I dismiss her concerns with a wave of my hand.

'I am fine. Nothing a good night's sleep won't put right. How is work going?' She sighs.

'I think I'm losing it, to be honest. I've made a couple of mistakes recently. Big ones. Things I'd never have done before. Plus, Young Mr Marchant is still being a knob.' I raise my eyebrows, as that is the closest to bad language I have ever heard Alice utter.

'What sort of mistakes?' She shakes her head.

'I won't bore you with the details, but it's seriously knocked my confidence. It's probably all to do with being menopausal.

135

I'm so forgetful nowadays.' I can see it is affecting her and my mind wanders to Rosie as I wonder if she is facing the same hormonal challenges.

A short while later, I leave and am glad to retreat to the sanctuary of home. Following Alice's comments, I look at myself in the mirror. Weight loss does your face no favours when you are older, and sure enough, it is telling. My cheekbones stand out where my cheeks have hollowed. My laughter lines, as Ned kindly called them, are much deeper. Also the shadows formed around my eyes from lack of sleep are hard to ignore.

Sunday – It is 49 years, 357 days since I last saw Rosie.

I have a big week coming up. Ned's funeral on Friday, the Murder Mystery on Saturday and, most importantly, Rosie's fiftieth birthday coinciding with Mother's Day on Sunday. Every time this comes to mind, a flutter of nerves rises in my stomach. Will she call? Is this the year?

In preparation, I do little for the rest of the weekend. I try to sleep, but it comes in fits and starts. Adrenaline surges each time I jolt awake. Cooking feels like too much effort, but I have run out of bread to toast, so manage a ready meal from the freezer for Sunday lunch.

Mostly I sit in my chair and, as I watch the world go by, I try to calm the thoughts that whirl through my mind. Those of Rosie dominate. Again, as so many times before, I remember the day I spent with her. The things I told her I wanted for her. I imagine her life since, her years drifting through my mind as I wonder if she was a happy child, a wilful teenager, if she did well at school and was career driven, or if she had a family.

Although supposedly nowadays you could manage it all and have both.

I think back with some regret to my plans of having a family. Maybe I let those dreams go too easily. Maybe I should have tried harder to find someone else to start again with, but at the time I was incapable of moving on. Of moving away from Rosie. As it is now, I have to face the reality she may never call. She may never want to know me.

Ned came along way too late for children. Plus, of course, he was married. At least with her condition, there was no chance his wife would be at the service. I would not go if there was. As it is, I can slip into a back row, pay my respects and leave without anyone knowing who I am.

I deliberate on whether I can face going to the Murder Mystery. Socialising is the last thing I want to do and I realise I have given up on attending all my clubs since Ned died. I have not given them a second thought. I have not sent my apologies and I have ignored all the emails that have come in regarding any of the activities I usually go to. Maybe it is time to give this one a miss, too. But then I feel bad about letting Sally down. We have made up a table between us, after all. And Alice is expecting me to watch her perform. Susannah Bugby too, come to that.

These thoughts and many more spark off each other, prickling through my mind like tiny bolts of lightning. One topic runs into another. Jumps about. Repeats. Back tracks. Repeats. Recovers old ground. Repeats. Guesses. Second-guesses. What's the right thing to do? What's wrong? No answers, never any answers. Just questions, questions, and more questions…

137

This is my weekend. I achieve nothing. Eat little. I am exhausted but cannot sleep. Cannot switch off. My mind is turbo-charged. All I do is sit, watch and drink.

19: The Start of the Big Week

Monday – It is 49 years, 358 days since I last saw Rosie.

I have to go to town to get my photos printed off. There is a chemist there with machines the public can use to do this. I remove the memory card from my camera and I drive to town, taking great care. It is not far, ten miles, and I made sure I stopped drinking early evening. But I am beyond exhausted and needed a couple of mugs of black coffee to pep me up for the journey.

I cannot remember the last time I drove anywhere, but as I have to get to the funeral on Friday, this will be good practice.

I am sure there are other errands I should be doing as I am going into town, but whatever they may be escapes me at present and the only thing I can focus on is getting the photos done.

The printing machines are available when I get to the shop. I hop up onto the stool in front of one of them and as I do so, the screen sways and I have to steady myself for a moment. Once the world rights itself again, I gaze at the machine and hope I can remember how to use it. It has been a while, and this has been another concern that has rattled through my brain over the last few days. Fortunately they turn out to be foolproof, which is just as well as I do not want to enlist the help of one of the shop assistants. They might think the subject of my photos a little odd, not being stunning scenery or cute children or pets.

I am soon heading back to the car with a packet of photos stowed away in my bag. I have made sure each one is date stamped with when it was taken, and once I get home I plan to add them into my journals to back up the notes I have made.

Tuesday and Wednesday

The problem with retirement is that there is an awful lot of time to fill. You do not appreciate it when you are working. Then there are never enough hours for you to do half what you want to. I had not noticed it before because of the lifestyle I adopted in joining all the societies and groups Amos and Evelyn belonged to. Now that I have stopped going and I am sleeping badly, the hours stretch out before me like shadows from a setting sun.

I try reading but cannot focus. Instead, I sit at my table with my journal and, out of habit, I keep my record of when Amos goes in or out. He is still going to the groups he has always attended, plus, of course, he has his new interests. I have decided I will report these to the police once this weekend is over. Mainly because I cannot face talking to them now. I have neither the strength, nor concentration. My mind cannot stay on one topic for more than a few seconds at a time. My hope is once I get past the funeral, the night out on Saturday and, managing my expectations, what I imagine will be another Mother's Day without my daughter everything will settle down and I will be able to sleep again. I am sure sleep is all I need and although the wine I have been drinking has made me drowsy, it has not helped knock me out in the way I had hoped. But that does not stop me from opening another bottle.

I know I am drinking too much. Usually, I hardly touch a drop but at moments of crisis this is what I have always done. The last time I drank like this was five years ago so it is hardly a frequent occurrence. Nothing to concern the doctors. For now, I need it. Alcohol dulls my pain. Softens the edges of my reality. I will drink to get through this week, this weekend, then I will stop. I have done it before. I can do it again.

In the meantime, I have still not got round to getting more milk and I am out of bread. There must be other things I need too. I look in the fridge and, faced with slime and furry mould, have to throw away most of the vegetables I bought. I simply have not been up to eating, let alone cooking.

I decide on the Wednesday morning to go to the coffee morning then pop to the shop afterwards to stock up before returning home. It is only when I push the door open to the hall, that I realise for the first time I do not have any cake to donate to the event. And I can hardly blame lack of time.

'Morning,' I say to Sally and Susannah as I pass them and head for the kitchen. There are a few others present already from the village, but I cannot face having to have a conversation with anyone. Sally follows me in and asks if I am alright.

'I am fine, thanks. I wish everyone would stop asking me that. It makes me afraid to step out of my home.'

'Sorry. We're worried. You're not your usual self.'

I flick on the kettle after filling it. 'No, well, I have got a lot on my mind.'

'Like what? Anything I can help with?' As she gets mugs out of a cupboard, I open one of the emergency variety packs of biscuits to hand out as I came empty-handed.

'Can you add these to the cakes already out there, please?'

'Why don't you go? It might do you good to talk to some other people.'

'You just asked if you could do anything to help and I have asked you to do this. I do not want to talk to anyone. If I did, I would do it myself.' Her hands rise in defence and a pang of guilt washes over me as she takes the biscuits and turns away to carry them out into the hall. It is not like me to snap, and I know she does not deserve it.

I soon get the chance to apologise as, after delivering the biscuits, she comes straight back in.

'Sorry,' I say, as she stands alongside, placing a hand on my shoulder by way of response before taking the first coffees out to the hall. I am glad she is happy to carry them. My hands are shaking too much today.

I leave as soon as I have done my bit, and as Sally and Susannah are chatting to others in the hall, I get out without further conversation.

I head straight for the shop, grab a basket on my way in and fill it quickly with milk, bread, and a few other essentials. Including a couple of bottles of wine to replenish my depleted stock. Last, I add all the vegetarian ready meals that there are in the chiller cabinet, hoping my appetite will soon be back. Sharon is on the till, naturally, and looks about as bad as I feel.

Astonishingly, for once she does not ask me to cover in the shop at any point. Our conversation doesn't stray beyond the words necessary to get through the sales process and I am soon on my way. My bags are heavy but I am pleased I have made the effort, as at least it means I have everything I need to see me through the weekend.

I am relieved to get back into my cottage. It is only when I have put everything away and pop to the bathroom that I glance in the mirror and see what everyone else has seen this morning.

I did not get round to putting on any makeup, nor brushing my hair before I went out and I look like something has dragged me through a hedge backwards. No wonder people don't think

I am coping. I tell myself I need to do better for the funeral and the Murder Mystery. However, right now what I need is a glass of wine and a sit down.

It is as I am lowering myself into my chair that I see Amos cross the road back to his cottage. I have not bothered to follow him this week, but I know he has just come from Agnes Peach's place. Dirty bugger. I cannot wait until the police are on his case.

20: The Police come Knocking

I have noticed this week that in the same way that I have counted the days of my life based on the last time I saw Rosie (49 years, 361 days), I also now describe time as how it is relative to Ned's demise. On the day before his funeral, there is a knock on the door. I already know who is there because I was in position to see the police car pull up outside. With no idea why the police are visiting and as it is never going to be good news, I ignore them. They must have the wrong house and will go away. Instead, they are more persistent than I expect. While the female officer stays out by the car and talks into her radio, the male one stands back and looks at the property, gazing at the windows upstairs, then as he peers in through the bay window, shades his eyes to cut out the reflection; I sit stock still as I watch from the other side of the nets. His presence makes my stomach lurch because I recognise him. At least I think I do. Is it him? Has he come for me? It occurs to me that if they get no answer, they may go to one of the neighbours, and I do not want that. It is bad enough to have police on the doorstep at all without more attention being drawn to them and the whispers starting.

I rake my fingers through my hair to tidy it, a sharp tug on my scalp as one catches in a knot.

I open the door enough to show my face and both officers turn towards me with some surprise and walk up the path. They introduce themselves and flash warrant cards, which I ignore. My initial reaction was right though. I do recognise him. We have met before, although nothing ever came of it. But my thoughts immediately jump to the fact that this is it, he has caught up with me at last.

Strangely, all I feel is relief.

'How can I help you?' I say, amazed at how calm my voice sounds.

'You are Miss Smith, aren't you? Miss Dora Smith.'

'Yes.'

'We've had a concern for welfare report and we're checking in to make sure you're okay. May we come in?'

He may be five years older than when we last met, but he still looks fresh out of school. Although he never went to my school, I would have remembered if he had. Interestingly, it appears he does not recognise me, so maybe my initial alarm was premature.

I look past the officers and see Amos standing in his front bay window, watching. I do not have to guess who made the call. Concern for welfare. What rubbish. It is typical behaviour of goody two shoes Amos to have stuck his nose into someone else's business. Just being a good neighbour. That is how he would defend his telling tales.

I open the door wider, stand back and without taking my eyes from Amos, usher them in, giving him a hard stare before closing it. They walk into the sitting room. I see them having a good look around. My jotter is open on the table. The binoculars nearby rest on the open pages of a photo album. Having gathered all my evidence against Amos, I wonder if I should mention my concerns about his behaviour to these two. But I dismiss the thought immediately. If he has sent them, they are already on his side and will never believe what I have to say. Tit for tat. That's what they will call it. I decide to stick to my plan and go to the station after the weekend.

'Shall we go through to the kitchen?' I lead the way so we can sit at the table, swiftly scooping the dirty dishes lying there onto the side by the sink where they join the others. I wet the dishcloth and wipe the tabletop, apologising for the mess. I thread the stems of three glasses, one still half full, between my fingers and scrub at the red wine rings they have left behind.

I place the glasses by the sink and turn back to see the female officer gazing at the unwashed ready meal cartons and plates.

'I have been busy.' I say this as dismissively as I can manage, as if it is perfectly normal for a woman like me to have two weeks' worth of washing up congealing on the side. 'Would you like a coffee?' Both decline, which is probably just as well as I am not sure there is a clean mug in the place.

As I sit, I look between them and say, 'What is this about? You say you have had a call?' My fingers twist in my lap and I pick at a rough edge of skin alongside my thumbnail.

She replies, 'Yes, a member of the public has raised a concern about your welfare, and we have a duty to make sure you're alright.' I smile and spread my hands wide.

'As you can see, I am perfectly fine.' Neither looks convinced. 'Who is this mysterious caller?'

'Obviously we can't divulge that information—'

'Of course, you can't,' I interrupt, but she perseveres.

'The caller told us they'd received an anonymous letter, and they thought you might have sent it.'

'Goodness, an anonymous caller and an anonymous letter? It sounds a bit farfetched. What did it say?'

It is his turn to speak. '"I know what you're doing".'

'That's it?' He nods.

'You will be telling me next it was made with cut out letters stuck to a page – all terribly Agatha Christie.' My attempt to make light of the situation falls flat.

'You've described it perfectly.'

'Oh.' Perhaps I should not have been frivolous. 'Well, maybe this mysterious caller should consider the contents of the letter, and perhaps think about their behaviour. The equally mysterious letter-sender presumably did not send it for no reason.' For the second time, I consider speaking to them about my concerns with Amos, but as it would confirm me as the letter-sender, again I decide against it.

His eyebrows rise. 'Oh. Can you think of why someone would have sent such a letter?'

I shake my head, keen not to incriminate myself. 'No, I cannot imagine anyone doing anything like that in a sleepy old village like this.'

She says, 'Are you coping alright, living on your own?' I see her eyes flick towards the dirty crockery and glasses again.

'Perfectly, thank you. I have always lived alone.'

'And you don't think you might need some extra help now?' *Bloody cheek.*

'No, I don't. Like I said, I have been busy.' I wave towards the mess. 'It is only a bit of washing up.'

She tilts her head as if in agreement, but I am not convinced by the act and I follow her eyes to the crumbs on the floor I had not noticed. I look at him and find him studying me. He clicks his fingers.

'We've met before. I knew you looked familiar.'

'We have. Five years ago.'

'Five years, was it? You've got an excellent memory.'

'It was a night that has been difficult to forget.' He nods, and I wonder if he remembers the incident or if it has been lost in all he has witnessed since. At least it appears not to be the reason he has turned up on my doorstep today. 'Well, if there is nothing else…' and I make a move to stand, 'it looks like I had better

147

get my washing up gloves on. Wouldn't want to get arrested for crimes against crockery.' My attempt at humour again falls flat, but I paste what I hope is a reassuring smile on my face and they take the hint, and both rise. He takes out a card and leaves it on the table.

'You can contact us if you need to.' I leave it where it is, mumbling my thanks to their backs as I follow them out.

He turns to face me once he is outside. 'Thank you for talking to us, Miss Smith.'

'Hopefully you are reassured I am perfectly alright and you can tell Amos Chamberlain he can keep his concerns to himself.' I hope the officer might give himself away, but he doesn't, each of us as cagey as the other. Closing the door before they are through the gate, I rush to my table, settling myself in my chair in case they cross the road to give feedback to Amos. But they are too wise to give away their informer and instead I watch them drive away. I glance around the room made messy with my paperwork strewn across every surface, and note the carpet could do with being reintroduced to the vacuum. But all that is for another day. For now, I have work to do.

I top up the half-full glass of wine, and settle back at my table before writing up my notes.

21: Another Funeral

I suppose at my age attending two funerals within a month cannot be considered unusual, although thankfully it is still a rarity rather than the norm. After my initial wobble, I do not give attending Ned's a second thought. Secret or not, it is the least I can do as his girlfriend, although of course I shall be discreet. I would not want to upset anyone. The crematorium is over twenty miles away because naturally Ned's family has arranged it close to his home. But they posted a notice with the details in Sharon's Stores and in the local paper so are presumably expecting some from the village to attend.

The journey is uneventful and as I left plenty of time, I am at the crematorium early. The car park is busy though, a constant flow of cars coming and going, such is the conveyor-belt nature of cremations. I sit and watch from my car keeping an eye on arrivals, keen to see if there is anyone I recognise.

To my surprise Sally Button arrives ten minutes later, Susannah Bugby a few minutes after that. It was not as if we had discussed it, and I immediately suspect they are here to keep an eye on me such has been their concern recently. This annoys me and I give no indication I have seen them. As the allotted time approaches, I exit the car and walk towards one of the ugliest buildings I have ever seen. Modern. Boxy. Unrelentingly grey. The columns that support an overhang industrial rather than aesthetic. Underfoot, embedded gravel in mesh provides an uneven surface for my heels and it is with relief that I reach the pavement.

'Wait up.' Sally Button is still doing up her coat as I turn and slow up enough to enable her to catch up with me. 'I didn't realise you were coming. I'd have given you a lift.' She lies easily. Playing the innocent.

'I was just thinking the same when you drove in.' I lie just as well. 'Susannah's here too.' She will know already, of course, they are collaborators after all.

'Oh, many others from the village?'

'Not that I have seen.' We are at the doors to the reception area of the crematorium. Or as I like to call it, the holding pen. People stand in ones or twos, sometimes small groups. There is a sign. *Ned Ladds* picked out in those removable letters under a framed photo. It is a good one. He is smiling. Relaxed. A pint glass on the picnic table he is sitting at. A pub garden somewhere, no doubt. I am saddened I never got to spend time with him in such a place.

'Aww, what a lovely photo,' Susannah Bugby says over my shoulder, her voice breathless. 'Do you think his wife will be here?'

'I wouldn't have thought so. Surely it would be too disruptive for her,' Sally replies.

'You're probably right.' We move away to the side so we are not blocking the photo for other mourners. I spot two women I recognise from either serving them in the shop or because their children were once at my school, but their names escape me. One dabs at her eyes with a tissue. The hearse draws up outside and I take a deep breath.

Someone opens the doors from the holding pen into a high-ceilinged chapel. Floor-to-ceiling windows down one side make it a bright space. A fake tan shade of wood lines the walls to halfway up, the rest painted in something from the dull end of the grey spectrum. There are only a few rows of chairs and I lead the way to one at the back to be out of the way. Order of

Service booklets are on every other seat, and I pick mine up before I sit. The same photo of Ned is on the cover, and I consider the fact that if I keep this, it is one of only a few I have of him. The others are on my phone. Grainy shots taken in my cottage. I flick through the booklet. Donations to a dementia charity. That is a nice touch. The two women I recognised from the holding pen fill the rest of our row.

I had prepared myself, should anyone ask, to say I am a client of Ned's. But now I am here, I am not sure it is a strong enough reason to attend someone's funeral. Maybe I should say I have been a client for many years. That he practically redecorated my entire house. Yes, that's it. That sounds much better. Reassured, I watch the seats fill, and a lump comes to my throat as we are asked to stand. My knees are so weak I am not sure I can.

Four pallbearers carry the coffin in and slide it, with a clatter, across the metal-studded top of the catafalque. The wood the coffin is constructed of is anaemic against the walls. A flower display in white and blue adorns the top. A fifth man follows and solemnly places Ned's photo at the end of the coffin.

The family enters. A couple of older women who I assume are his sisters, their arms linked at the elbows. Then three couples in their forties. I know he had three children and there are five youngsters who I take to be grandchildren. One of the oldest, a teenage girl with red-rimmed eyes, sniffs. They fill the front rows.

Sally rifles in her bag beside me and withdraws a tissue, which she does little with other than scrunch it up in her hand.

The celebrant is a young man and as soon as he speaks I take against him. I understand it is most likely he never met Ned, but from the way he talks, I suspect he has also had little more than a passing conversation with Ned's family. Or more likely nowadays he has dealt with putting together the whole service by email. He reads from a script I imagine he has already repeated several times today. His reedy voice, thin and nasal, manages to sound both bored and hurried. He rushes through the entire service, although I imagine the crematorium markets it as efficient.

There is little to inspire emotion. Although that does not stop the woman at the end of our row from sobbing throughout.

There are a few interesting details about Ned and his wife, Christine's, life together. I only realise now Ned never used her name as it is the first time I have heard it. I wonder if she knows he has died and if once told she remembers that information or if she has to keep being told. How horrible for her family, if that is the case.

It feels like no sooner have we sat down than we are invited to join the family for tea and refreshments and as Frank Sinatra's 'My Way' starts up, we are once more on the move through doors leading to a small courtyard.

I know the crematorium is run with efficiency but I am not sure I like this slick method of dealing with the dead. It is while my thoughts still dwell on this topic that I am taken off guard and make a mistake.

On my way through the exit doors, I had decided I was going to go straight home. But…

'I could do with a cup of tea,' says Susannah. 'You coming?' She is asking both Sally and me, but as I shake my head Sally says she needs to use the facilities anyway, so she might as well. What I should have done was stick to my original plan, but Sally says,

'You should join us, Dora. What are you rushing back for?'
What indeed? It is always at this point I wish I had a dog or something needing my attention, but I do not, and they know it.

'Oh, go on then.' My reluctance is obvious but with as little persuasion as that, while I feel the pull of my car, I turn away and head for a flat-roofed cuboid shaped building in the corner of the car park. A short while later we stand together near the sobbing woman, who has now fortunately stopped, and her friend, holding lukewarm teacups of insipid tea and with little to say. It seems ridiculous for us to exchange stories of Ned, as encouraged by the celebrant, because for us all he was our handy man, therefore I search for another topic.

'Are you still up for the Murder Mystery?' I ask Sally, as she is good at taking in the detail at the event. Like me, she makes notes.

'I'm looking forward to it. Are the others all confirmed?'

'Yes, Laura, Harry, Olivia, and Kyle. Pip cannot make it. I hope they don't mind being with us oldies.'

'They'd have made an excuse if they did.'

Susannah says, 'I'm one of the suspects.' We already know this otherwise she would probably be on our table. But the members of M.A.T.S. who make up the six suspects for the evening, together with the lead investigator, DCI O'Nonotagain, the one consistent character, sit together on their self-appointed top table. They then behave theatrically all evening although Amos Chamberlain, their leader and cast organiser, would say they were merely staying in character.

'Ahh, of course. What part are you playing?'

'Ooh, you can't trick me – no clues ahead of the night.' She wags her finger at me.

'I don't think it counts as a clue, Susannah, as you all get introduced at the start of the evening.'

'Oh yes, of course we do. Silly me. All right then, I'm Georgie Thorn. A writer of thrillers.' As this year's Murder Mystery is called *The Poison Pen* on all the marketing, I had already assumed the literary connection.

'Sounds good. Have you learned your lines?' Susannah wrinkles her nose and as I glance across the room, I see one of the older women from Ned's family group break away and walk in our direction. It is the first time I have seen her face-on and she is striking. Attractively made up, she is wearing a beautifully cut dress. Her figure is slim and graceful. As she approaches, I wish I had acted on my initial desire and was already on my way home, as the thought of having to hold a conversation with a family member is not appealing. I try to concentrate on Susannah's reply while keeping an eye on the woman, who does not look particularly grief-stricken as she exchanges a few words with another person, then laughs as she pats them on the arm. The level of background noise means I could hear nothing of what was being said.

'We all have a script on hand to make sure we've given everyone all the clues so no lines to be learned, thank goodness.' Distracted, I nod along to her reply whilst realising I have already asked Alice this question and got the same answer. Just as well she is not here or it would give her another reason to be concerned about me.

The woman joins our group. She exudes confidence. Her eyes sparkle.

'Hello.' She addresses us all. 'I'm Christine. Ned's wife. We haven't met, but I assume you are his girlfriends. So good of you to come along.' And just like that, the oxygen is sucked from the room.

Christine. Most definitely not in a care home debilitated by dementia then.

'What?' Sally says, her voice squeaky. All my strength drains from me, as Susannah's face blanches. I glance around, anxious to ensure no one is close enough to have overheard.

'I am sorry, er, Christine, was it?' My voice cracks on her name and I have to clear my throat to continue. 'I think there must be some mistake. I was a customer of Ned's for many years. He practically redecorated my entire house.' While this sounds like I am reading from a script, Sally and Susannah both nod their heads and make similar mumblings.

'Don't be silly, dear. The fact my husband was a dab hand with a paintbrush is not what brought you here today. I know all about you. Or at least I know of your existence, which…' and she pauses as she looks around the group, narrowing her eyes as she manages to include the other two ladies as well, 'I think is rather more than any of you knew about each other. Am I right?' She claps her hands as if in delight. My mouth dries as I glance at Sally and Susannah, who look as horrified as I feel. I can't believe they were also seeing him. Sleeping with him. It can't be true? Confused, I think this must be a joke. Although why would Christine make something like that up? Even as this thought crosses my mind, I know I have to stop kidding myself. Of course, it's true. Reality hits, and, as my spirits plummet, I realise that Ned, dear, sweet, trustworthy Ned, has duped us all.

'You don't seem cross?' I struggle to get my words out, while wishing the ground would open beneath me, but have to ask because she seems to be positively glowing about the whole mortifying revelation.

'Oh, I'm not.' She shakes her head to reinforce her words. 'Ned and I have had an open relationship for years. He's a naughty boy though because he's clearly never told any of you,' and as she casts her eye across the stunned group again, the sobbing one breaks down completely. 'Aww.' Christine reaches out and places a hand on her arm in comfort. 'I'm guessing you were the one he died on top of.' As the woman howls and runs from the room closely followed by her friend, Christine almost clucks in sympathy. 'Poor woman. That's not a nice thing to happen, is it?' I assume she is not actually expecting an answer, as faced with the reality of how he died, my cheeks flush with heat.

Susannah leans in. 'You're looking, um, a lot healthier than Ned led me to believe you were.' It is my turn to nod this time.

'Oh, what did he tell you, cancer? Something horribly long lasting and inevitably terminal?'

'Early onset dementia.' Sally's voice is so weak we all crane to hear it. Christine screws up her face.

'Oooh, nasty. But it doesn't surprise me. Gets the sympathy card, doesn't it? Plus,' and she clicks her fingers as if the answer has only then come to her, 'I bet that's how he got you all to be discreet about your relationship. Another bonus being he didn't have to fork out on wining and dining you.' She laughs lightly. 'You've got to hand it to him. He had it all worked out.'

He did indeed.

This is honestly the weirdest conversation I have ever been part of. It is so weird, in fact, I have not even begun to process everything I have learned. At this point, the other older woman crosses the room towards us as I say to Christine, 'You seem quite happy with how he was living and behaving.' The other woman reaches Christine's side, threads a many-bangled arm through her elbow again. There is something more sensual and less sisterly in the act than I noticed earlier.

'Oh, yes. Like I said, we had an open relationship, but I am not a randy old goat like Ned and found my happy place a few years ago with this one.' She smiles into the eyes of the other woman. They kiss. A touch of lips, nothing more. Christine turns back towards us, 'Of course, it never stopped Ned from joining us in bed on more than a few occasions.' She grins and her lover does likewise. 'He will be much missed. But however sad we have been over his passing no one can say he didn't live his life to the full.' I close my mouth, fearful it might be gaping as she finishes, 'Anyway, lovely to meet you all. Have a safe journey home. Melton, isn't it?' And having apparently completed her revelations she turns with her girlfriend, and they wander down between the tables to where the buffet awaits.

Already struggling with my appetite, I fear anything I eat now would make a swift reappearance. I have to leave, and without a word to either of the others, I place my teacup on the nearest table and head for the door with as much dignity as I can muster.

I am halfway across the car park before they catch up with me.

'Stop,' says Sally, and she places her hand on my upper arm to reinforce her request. I turn. See Susannah is not far behind.

'What do you want?'

'Just to talk. To discuss what we do now.'

'What we do now? Nothing, that's what. We do nothing. We say nothing to anyone. He has made a fool of us all and I do not want this getting out. We will be a laughing stock.'

'It won't be that bad,' says Susannah, in some lame attempt to console.

'It will be.' I jab my finger towards her to emphasise my point. 'I will also be getting a complete health check at the doctors. God only knows what he has been spreading about.'

'Hey, what are you implying? He didn't catch anything from me, if that's what you're getting at.'

'I am not saying he did, and I am certainly not blaming anyone. But I trusted him when I shouldn't have. And I suspect you both did, too.' The looks on their faces told me everything I needed to know. Sally gave a long sigh.

'She's right,' she says to Susannah. 'We should get checked out.'

'Right. We do that and we say nothing to anyone about what's happened.' They nod in unison.

'But,' and Sally hesitates, 'I think he already had a reputation in the village. I think some people knew what he was up to. I have heard a few things over the years. Some hints, you know. The word might be out already.'

'Why didn't you say something before?'

She looks uncomfortable, her eyes sliding away from mine, 'It's not the sort of thing you do mention, is it? We're not in the habit of discussing our sex lives, or lack of them.'

I am reminded of the conversations I had with Kyle, Sharon and Alice. The things they said, the suspicions they raised. 'And you didn't think to challenge him on it?'

'No, I was having a good time. I didn't want it to end.'

Susannah nods along. 'I've thought before that people knew he was a ladies' man.' Their inaction in not exposing him exasperates me. Or maybe it is because it exacerbates just how foolish I feel that I find it irritating. I did not suspect he was up to anything. I thought he was all mine, which just goes to show what a complete idiot I have been.

'We say nothing to confirm any gossip or suspicions. Got it?' They both nod.

Sally adds, 'But what about the other woman? The one who, well, you know, he was with when he died?'

'Do you honestly think she is going to say anything? Look, we keep quiet. We do not even mention we came to this funeral. And as far as anyone knows, Ned only did work for us.'

'The bugger had the cheek to charge for it, too.' Sally is right and for the first time, I see anger building up in her. 'I can't believe he played us like this.'

'And when I think about all the times I cooked for him because he had no one at home to do it. What a bastard.' Susannah now looks as irritated as Sally, and I think about all the times I fed him too and can only sympathise. But I am not angry. I wish I were. I am feeling something else entirely and need to be alone, so I say my goodbyes and continue on my journey to the car. Each step is now more laboured than the last as the enormity of what has happened hits home.

My eyes brim with tears, as I start the car with shaking hands, and I have to keep wiping them away the entire journey. Sadness grows along with an increasing level of shame the closer I get to Melton.

I park outside my cottage, let myself in and once the door is firmly closed behind me, I grab a cushion from the sofa, hold it tight across my face and scream into it. By the time I pull it away from my face again, I am shaking, tears falling as the depth of my disappointment and hurt plunges to new levels.

I have been betrayed by someone I was in love with. And not for the first time. I think about the tears I shed when I heard he had died, and feel foolish. He must have been laughing at us all.

Playing us. Turning from one to the other. All so willing. So gullible. So desperate were we to be loved.

I empty a bottle of wine into a glass and down the contents, carry another from the kitchen and climb the stairs. Breaking the seal I take a long drink, not bothering with a glass, then kick off my heels and crawl under the duvet. Night closes in as I work my way through the bottle and I wonder if this will be what kills me. This final humiliation.

22: The Poison Pen

I wake in the morning fully clothed. My hand is clamped around the neck of the empty bottle and despite the evidence to the contrary I feel like I have not slept a wink. The pounding in my head intensifies at the slightest movement. My mouth is dry, like the gritty floor of a birdcage. I reluctantly get out of bed and shuffle through to the bathroom to relieve myself. The sight in the mirror is not a pretty one. The lines around my eyes are accentuated by the makeup creased into them. My hair is a tousled mess. I consider my options and, after drinking some water and taking a couple of pills for my head, decide to go back to bed. A first for me.

I am barely settled when my phone pings. A text from Sally Button.

You'd better not be having second thoughts about coming tonight.

No second thoughts, no. It had been my first thought on waking. After the fact that it is 49 years, 363 days since I last saw Rosie.

I text back:

I am not sure I am up for it.

The next moment, she is on the phone.

'It will raise everyone's suspicions if you're not there. You've been behaving weirdly enough anyway and if you don't come tonight, they'll know something's wrong and it will inevitably come out about Ned. You were the one keen on keeping it quiet.'

She is right, I had not thought about the consequences. I sigh, reluctance clear in my response.

'All right, I will be there.'

'That's the spirit.' She hangs up and I continue to lie in bed. Fully dressed. Thankfully, despite it being Saturday, Alice will not be round this morning as she is at the village hall with the rest of the cast preparing for tonight. Resigned to having to face the village this evening and not wanting to spend the day fretting about it, I decide I have nothing to get up for so lie staring vacantly at the wall.

Tomorrow it is Rosie's fiftieth birthday. I vow once I get home after the Murder Mystery, I will not have another drop to drink until I get to talk to her tomorrow. I want to be clearheaded, focused and completely in the moment for when the call comes in. And it must do. Surely. Mother's Day. Her fiftieth. As I have asked myself countless times over the last few months. If not now, then when?

The elusiveness of decent sleep recently has caught up with me and I doze, but jerk awake early afternoon in no way refreshed. It takes me a few moments to remember why I am still in bed and in my funeral dress. My headache has gone though, which is something. I get up and go to run myself a bath. As I lie in it later and contemplate the state of my aged body, I cannot help but think of Ned and how much I enjoyed my relationship with him. Despite the way he deceived me and many others, I already miss the life I had with him, such as it was. And I know I will miss being in love with him.

162

I remember when he redid my kitchen. I had had two weeks of Ned being there every day. The closest I have ever come to living with someone. Which, in retrospect, is a tad sad. I loved those two weeks though, and had enjoyed the opportunity to look after someone. Despite the challenges of not having a proper kitchen to work in, I had provided lunch every day and tempted him into staying longer by offering dinner, too. "It'll save you having to get something for yourself," I had said, and I had been sorry for the fact he would be returning each night to an empty house. What a fool I was. When I think about that time now, I remember the afternoons when he would disappear off for a couple of hours muttering about needing supplies. I realise now with the benefit of hindsight he had actually been keeping his other women happy.

It was amazing he got away with it for this long. Juggling women as he did. And with some of us in such proximity. But Sally was quite right, it is not something you talk about, is it? Your sex life. Especially when Ned had spun us all the story of his poor sick wife in a care home. And how he hated the thought of betraying her, and his family, by them finding out he had found love elsewhere.

Love.

I wonder if he knew the meaning of the word, although he talked a good talk.

I got the distinct impression yesterday that for Sally and Susannah Ned had been a bit of fun and something not to be taken too seriously. For me, he was so much more. I was ill-equipped for anything casual. And, it appeared, incapable of simply sleeping with someone for a bit of fun. Admittedly, I had only slept with two men in my life, but I had fallen in love with them both. The thought that no one would ever love me, or at

163

least love my body, the way he had, ever again, brought more tears at his loss. For who would want to make love with me now? It saddened me to think that side of my life was at an end.

I arrive at the village hall shortly after seven. I had a glass of wine before I left to take the edge off my nerves, plus one in the bath now I come to think of it, but I have an unopened bottle with me as there is no licence for tonight's event therefore it is bring-your-own.

The hall is already heaving with people. As I enter, I spot the cast for the evening gathered around their table up on the stage. Flamboyantly dressed and in character is Susannah Bugby as thriller writer Georgie Thorn, dramatically dressed in black. Heavy kohl eye makeup completes her Goth like appearance, broken only by the chunky jewellery she wears. Her necklace and several bangles are in various shades of green. Whereas Alice Fraser is more conservatively dressed in one of her business suits, much like she is every day. Although she has added a large pair of glasses which give her an owlish appearance. When I reach my table, I glance at the cast list to find she is playing Alice Tregorran, who provides administrative support to the owner of the fictitious Tilman House Publishing, Matthew Tilman. So completely typecast, Amos hasn't even bothered to change her first name.

The format for these events has remained unchanged over several years. First there is the introduction of the suspects, a handy list of whom is on each table. We, the audience for the evening, are the sleuths and must work out who carried out the murder, how they did it and why.

There are three rounds where the suspects divulge information and the sleuths ask questions. They fit all this around a three-course meal. If you are a serious sleuth, which as previously mentioned I am, the food is secondary to the actual concentration on and working out of the clues.

The other members of my table are in their seats and sorting out their drinks. We exchange greetings and I am annoyed to realise the only chair left is next to Sally. This is where I would usually sit, but tonight her presence makes me feel awkward and I could have done with some separation. Olivia Croxton leans across her husband Kyle, to pour the contents of a large packet of crisps into a bowl in the centre of the table.

'In case anyone's peckish,' she says, helping herself to a handful before plopping back down on her seat. Harry O'Connor does likewise, grinning at Laura Brown next to him.

'You're never not hungry,' she says.

'That's because you work me so hard.' She shakes her head and reaches to help herself. Laura owns the stable yard and Harry works for her, as well as other places. It is a shame Pip, who ran all the riding lessons, couldn't come along, but she is rarely out in the evening for one so young.

'You okay?' Sally speaks quietly and without looking at me. I follow suit when I reply.

'Absolutely terrific.'

Barry Jones is on his feet and calls for quiet. He looks remarkable, dressed in a tweed cape-like coat and deerstalker hat. I suspect neither will remain on for long given the number of people in the room and how hot I know the hall will get. I offer my wine around the table, but everyone already has a drink, so I pour myself a glass and settle back to concentrate on what Barry has to say.

He and his wife Cordelia live in the biggest house in the village, if you discount Melton Manor. The Grange is set up a long drive. When the Joneses moved in, which must be ten or fifteen years ago now, they spent a considerable sum renovating the house and landscaping the gardens. Not that anyone has seen either as they keep themselves to themselves. Barry is a somewhat surprising recent addition to M.A.T.S. and I am led to believe by Alice he is fine in whatever part they give him as long as he gets to play himself.

Of his wife there is no sign this evening. This does not surprise me. Barry has worked away for long periods of time in a highly pressured job in order to keep her in the manner she expects, but he is now nearing retirement. Consequently he is taking life easier and is therefore more present in the village, his joining M.A.T.S. one example of that. Cordelia meanwhile remains as aloof as ever and unsupportive. Of course, one of the few conversations we have had when the subject of surnames came up may have jaded my view of her. She declared the only thing possibly worse than her taking Barry's common-as-muck surname, Jones, would have been if it had been Smith. The fact she was talking to a Smith completely passed her by. I remember her peals of laughter when she described Barry's hurt when she had told him she would not take his name when they married. She had naturally double-barrelled it instead, well before it was trendy, of course, and had ended up as Cordelia Hampton-Jones.

I did not care for her.

Although I had enjoyed watching her flinch on the odd occasion in the past when Barry had been referred to as Bazza in her presence.

Barry introduces himself as Detective Chief Inspector O'Nonotagain and says we have a mysterious death to investigate before he sets out the premise for the evening. The writers, and he gesticulates towards those sitting on the suspects' table, published by Tilman House Publishing, have been invited by Matthew Tilman to the annual dinner which is held at a local swanky restaurant. The purpose of the event is for Matthew Tilman to thank his writers for their work over the past year and to exhort them to greater efforts in the future. For the writers, they see it as an opportunity to remind Tilman they exist and have families to support and bills to pay.

Barry tells us Ted Fadds, being something of a curiosity as he is a male writer in the female dominated world of romantic suspense, has not turned up despite accepting the invitation. When a car was sent round to his apartment, the driver found the place locked, but on looking through the letterbox could see a light on inside. There was no answer to his repeated knocking, so he had summoned the caretaker, who opened the door with his master key. They found Ted dead, lying face down in his study. The police had been called, and they quickly established the time of death as some days before. Due to the "locked room" nature of the death and Ted's limited circle of friends, the finger of suspicion has fallen on the Tilman House Publishing writers' group and DCI O'Nonotagain has arrived to quiz the suspects. Anticipating some elaborate storytelling, he enlists the help of all the sleuths present to unmask the guilty party.

Barry introduces Matthew Tilman, played by Jeremy Cross, who I note is in a wheelchair.

As he wheels himself to face the room, I ask Sally, 'What happened to Jeremy?'

'The official story is he broke his leg skiing.' She keeps her voice low.

'And the unofficial?'

'The village believes he did it during a rather athletic sex act.'

'Oh.' This is the problem with being someone who does not spread gossip. It is often not shared with you. Sally stifles a giggle as she raises her eyebrows at me.

Jeremy's delivery is stilted as he says, 'Hello, yes, I'm Matthew Tilman, owner of Tilman House Publishing. Well, this disaster could finish Tilman House. Although, I suppose one shouldn't be too hasty. Ted's new book is ready to print and some exposure for it in the national dailies might make all the difference. After all, they do say there's nothing like a dead author to increase sales…' there are a few theatrical boos in the room, but not put off Jeremy continues, 'Oh… too soon? Hmm. Perhaps I should make a few calls when this night is over. Oh, Ted's book? It's called *The Poison Pen Club*… you'll find it in all good bookshops.'

Susannah Bugby is introduced as thriller writer Georgie Thorn. 'You've probably read some of my novels: *The Train of the Dead, The Surgeon's Knife, The Valley of Blood*? No? Oh well, never mind. They're all still available wherever you buy your books.

'I can't say I was a fan of Ted. We are… or were rivals for the chair of the Writers' Group. I thought him rude and a boor, and I didn't much care for his work either. Those romantic suspense stories are terribly one-dimensional and the sex badly written. I could have done better, of course, but wouldn't lower myself. Typical of him to snatch the limelight though, selfish man.'

Alice Fraser is primed and, carrying a clipboard to make her more officious, gets to her feet without Barry having to nudge her. 'I'm Alice Tregorran, and I run Tilman House Publishing. Well, Matthew obviously runs it, but I do everything else. I do the bookkeeping, open the post, sort out launch parties and publicity, pay writers their royalties and expenses, run errands for Matthew, answer the phone when he's not there and often when he is. I also organise the website which will have to be updated with today's news, as if I haven't got enough to do. I suppose Ted was my least favourite of the authors. Such a demanding man, and always fiddling his expenses.'

Amos Chamberlain, wearing a smoking jacket and cravat with a copy of, presumably, his character's book under his arm, stands the minute Alice has finished to introduce himself as Rafe S. Chevalier, a distinguished writer of travel guides. I cannot help but smile to myself. He always gives himself such pompous roles and names. As typecast as poor Alice, in a way.

He continues, 'Have you read any of my travel guides? No? I happen to have a copy here,' and he brandishes the book previously under his arm, 'if anyone cares to take a look. It's sad to hear that Ted Fadds, with whom I have shared many a writer's research adventure, is no longer with us. A sad day indeed. I suppose it must be suicide, of course.'

Petula Cross, clearly not wanting to be outdone in the acting stakes, leaps to her sandal-clad feet (I have never seen Petula out of heels before) her ragged-edged long layered skirts swishing about her legs. Dramatically, she throws her shawl round and over her shoulder before saying, 'Oh my goodness, who would have thought Ted would do such a thing? Suicide? Surely not. It must have been an accident, mustn't it? I know he had money problems; I could never get a penny out of him. I'm sorry, I haven't introduced myself. I'm Flora Myth, earth mother and writer of second chance romance.'

I have never heard of such a thing as second chance romance. It sounds terribly niche.

Too long a silence follows, during which Barry stares at the last suspect, who in real life is Eddie Lumbers, indicating by jerking his head for him to follow suit. Eddie looks horrified at the prospect. Alice had told me Amos had struggled to get his cast together this year. It appears he has roped in Eddie, who is more usually to be found as a stagehand at a M.A.T.S. performance. I cannot help but wonder how much the fact Alice was already in the cast had influenced Eddie's decision to take part.

At last Eddie is on his feet and shuffles forward, his introduction monotone. 'I'm science fiction writer Zac Preston. I guess that's the last chapter for poor old Ted. There'll never be another one like him, thank God. I can't imagine there'll be much of a rush to write his obituary although, knowing Alice, it's already in the just-in-case file. Typical of a suspense writer to get himself centre stage in a locked room mystery. However, I suppose we can all be grateful the romance element was not part of his death. Mind you, it certainly played a major role in his life.' He takes his seat again with some relief.

Eddie, as Zac Preston, has done his best to look smart in a jacket and tie yet still manages to be scruffy and out of place. Which probably reflects how Eddie is feeling. He also keeps tapping a cigarette on the table, bringing it to his lips before realising it is a non-smoking venue.

At this point, all the suspects stand and approach us, the audience, or sleuths, spreading out among the tables. Round One has begun, and the game is afoot.

During the three rounds, each of the suspects divulges various pieces of information at all the tables of sleuths. As there are six suspects and each one makes three or four different statements in each round, you can imagine there are a lot of red herrings. The skill is in picking out the facts of importance. Naturally, that is easier if you keep a clear head and Kyle has already leaned over to refill my glass. Among others, I should add.

During the next twenty minutes, each of the suspects visits our table and imparts the pieces of information they need to share. None of them do this without referring to a prompt in some way, although Alice's clipboard is the most discreet method and I listen when she tells us Ted was always considered mysterious. With the other authors, she knew when spouses' birthdays were, or when their children passed a milestone, and made a point of sending small gifts, so everyone felt appreciated, but she didn't even know if Ted had a family. I try to concentrate on the detail but as the events of yesterday weigh heavily on my mind, I struggle.

We hear all sorts from the suspects; from issues with Ted at university to the fact that Tilman House Publishing is in financial trouble. Road accidents, competition for who was going to stand as chairperson of the writers' group, and raunchy goings-on during research trips away with authors who were collaborating on work, were just some of the clues dropped by the suspects.

Sally pays better attention than me, and I see she is making her usual notes. Even Olivia jumps in to ask a couple of questions while I reach for some crisps to put something in my stomach.

Once the first round is over, the village hall band of organisers bring the starter out. Pâté and toast. There appears to be no vegetarian option so I eat the toast as if I am starving. Although, as I do, I realise it is the first thing I have eaten today, other than the few crisps. No wonder the wine has gone to my head. I do not taste the food so much as inhale it.

The noise level in the hall is such that no one nearby can possibly overhear when Sally starts to discuss the various clues the suspects had given us. The rest of the team are considerably more interested than me in favouring or discounting various options. The new members do not notice, but my lack of participation does not get past Sally.

'Wake up, Dora. What's wrong with you tonight?' Then she says to the rest of those round the table, 'She's usually all over the clues like a regular Miss Marple.'

'Sorry. I didn't sleep well last night.' My smile is apologetic. 'I will try to do better in the next round.' My glass is full; I take a sip and glance across at Sally's notes, at least feigning interest.

The second round is much like the first. A deluge of information. But I pick my way through the details and manage to assist Sally with her notes. My cheeks are warm and no doubt pink and realising how hot it is in the room I take my cardigan off, which brings a brief respite. I am also thirsty and could do with some water, but there is none on the table. I look round the room.

'What are you looking for?' Harry asks.

'Water. I don't know if there are any jugs anywhere.'

'I'm sure I can get one from the kitchen.' He gets up and as I meanwhile drain my glass, Laura leans across to check Sally's notes.

'I'm sure it has something to do with Georgie Thorn's new book, *Fangs of the Python*. The writers are all being a lot bitchier about each other this round, don't you think?'

Jeremy, as Matthew Tilman, has rolled up to our table, and because of the noise we all have to lean in to hear the

172

information he needs to share. He denies any possibility his publishing house is in financial trouble, although admits business is tough. Still, a bestseller with Ted's latest will help. He continues with the fact that Alice is, of course, a treasure and has organised the whole writers' dinner then he says, 'You know there were always whispers about Ted, sometimes more than that, about him being a bit of a ladies' man – know what I mean?' And he gives us a lecherous wink. 'We certainly knew he worked his way through any female writers he encountered – lucky bugger. Quite honestly, I don't know what they saw in him, but I heard he had them on some sort of rota. What a lad!' Jeremy chortles as if this is funny.

What a lad!

The phrase echoes in my mind long after Jeremy struggles up the ramp to rejoin the top table, his work done for the time being.

While the others discuss the latest clues, I pretend to be interested but remain silent, my mind on another train of thought completely.

We have reached the main course part of the evening. A cottage pie is delivered to each table and Olivia serves it up onto the plates before passing them round. Steam rises from the separate vegetarian portion placed in front of me, but the toast was all that was needed to sate my appetite.

Kyle has filled my glass again. Drinking is considerably more appealing than eating as I consider what I think I know and wonder if I am reading more into things than are actually there. I nudge Sally and she looks across at me, her mouth full, but one eyebrow raised in question.

'Have you noticed the name thing?' I ask. She frowns, shakes her head. I reach to pull the list of the suspects towards us. My finger underlines the name Ted Fadds. 'Remind you of anyone?' She shakes her head again. 'Think about what Jeremy just told us.'

'Matthew Tilman.'

'Whatever.' Irritation flares at the correction. I think Sally senses it because, as though she's appeasing me, she takes the list and concentrates on it for a moment.

'Oh dear. You mean Ted Fadds is Ned Ladds.' I nod, unable to speak. 'Well, it doesn't matter, does it? So what if they added him in for a bit of local colour?'

'It is tasteless.'

Sally tries to be reassuring. 'Amos wrote this months ago. It was probably too late to come up with a different plot. Plus, it's not like he actually came from the village. I daresay most people won't even notice.'

'What about what Jeremy said about him having his women on a rota? We may have suspected people might have known but that is like someone definitely knew what he was up to.'

'Maybe, but Ned wasn't a writer, was he? Maybe it's simply a coincidence.' She smiles hopefully at me.

'It would have been a dead giveaway, wouldn't it, if the cast had turned up in a range of decorators' overalls, were attending a home exhibition at the nearest convention centre and the evening was billed as *The Painter's Plot*?' My words come out harsher than I intend them to be and I see Sally is uncomfortable. 'Someone knows, Sally. The someone who wrote this mystery.' She grimaces.

'Amos then.'

I sit back in my chair heavily. 'Well, that's just bloody brilliant, isn't it?'

174

My veggie pie remains untouched, and Kyle asks me if I want it. I wave it away, knowing it would choke me if I tried it.

I look over at the suspects' table and meet Amos' gaze, which is unusual. He has spent decades avoiding such direct contact. Although I caution myself not to read anything into it, I know I am not imagining the twisted smile on his lips.

This is his doing. This Murder Mystery plot. The rhyming of Ned's name. I bring myself up short. Look back at the cast list. Run my finger down the characters, but I cannot see any other connection or rhyme until I get to Flora Myth. Of course. Dora Smith. I look back to where Amos sits, and he is still watching me. He must be loving every moment as I work this out. He has been clever, I will give him that. It is a sub-plot in the storyline of the Murder Mystery, put in there purely to humiliate me, of that I am sure, and as I wonder if anyone else has noticed I glance round at the other tables.

A couple of people catch my eye. I see one woman nudge her neighbour and cock her head in my direction. They giggle conspiratorially. My heart flutters, my breaths shallow, and as I consider with shame what this evening could reveal, heat flushes my cheeks.

What a lad! Of course, that's why Jeremy added those words. A small clue to Ned Ladds. And if he had said them at every table; well, people would soon put two and two together.

Sally said Amos had written this months ago. Which was most likely true. Had Ned not died, this could quite possibly have been an evening of revelation for me. One along the lines of what I suffered at the funeral yesterday. As it was, he had died and if Amos had any compassion, he could have easily changed the names, maybe rephrased the clues to not make that

175

much of Ned's tomcatting around. But he chose not to. He chose to be spiteful and expose my humiliation to the village instead.

Once upon a time I had expected many things of my future husband. A propensity for cruelty was not one of them.

I drain my glass as I gaze at Petula in her Flora Myth guise as she approaches our table, and see what I hadn't before. The bag slung over her shoulder. The contents causing the top to gape so they are on full view. A soft toy, a couple of nappies, a muslin, a bottle. There's a dummy too, pinned to one side.

I look again for Amos, but he is busy spinning his lies to another table.

How could he know?

An ache joins the emptiness which never leaves my heart. A blanket. Pink. I reach to touch its unbearable softness against my skin.

I lean away, and towards Sally, who's hanging on Petula's every word.

'He knows about the baby,' I say from the corner of my mouth.

'What?' She sounds impatient.

'The baby. There's a baby.'

'Of course there's a baby. We've had that piece of information already. Where's your head at this evening, Dora?' She's quite right. I can't concentrate. Not heard a word, Petula, as Flora had to say.

'Does he know who the father is? Does he go that far?'

'That far?' Sally straightens, looks puzzled. 'What are you talking about?'

I ignore the question because he's out to get me. I know that now.

And I have to confront him.

176

Stop him.

I jerk round in my seat to see where he is and find Rafe S. Chevalier is currently entertaining the table behind ours. Unable to wait for him to finish and move on to us, I stand. My chair tips back and clatters to the floor. The noise is enough for those around us to notice the disturbance.

'You,' I say, pointing a finger in Amos's direction. 'Why are you doing this?'

He turns, spreads his arms wide, palms up, like he is innocent. 'Doing what?'

I gesticulate around the room, drawing more attention. 'All this.' He frowns, but there's something underneath, the glimmer of a smile, a smirk I don't care for. He goads me.

'You've been to plenty before, Dora. It's a Murder Mystery. A made-up story.' He says this slowly, as if he's talking to someone who has trouble understanding.

'Made up! Made up!' My voice rises with frustration. 'There is nothing made up about this.'

'Oh? I don't know what you mean? Enlighten me.' He's loving every moment. I can see it in the glint that comes to his eyes. The room grows quiet. I feel Sally's hand on my shoulder, but I brush it away.

'The names.'

He shrugs, like he doesn't know what I'm talking about. I should stop now. It's what he expects. I should sit down. Be quiet. Go back to being Dora Smith, the mild-mannered little old lady everyone knows, but it's too late. Anger spikes.

'Ted Fadds and Flora Myth. Really? Is that the best you could do?'

'Probably not, but it's done the trick. Don't you think?' He exhales, looks as if he's about to walk away, but turns back.

'Look, it's a bit of fun, Dora. Calm down.' Like those two words ever calmed anyone down. Rage floods my veins.

'A bit of fun? You're messing with people's lives, Amos. It's cruel. He's only just died.'

I hear someone say, 'Oh shit,' off to my right, like they'd only just then realised. A rustle of whispers follows, but my gaze never wavers from Amos.

'I admit the timing isn't great, but I couldn't do anything this late on.'

'You could. You could have changed the names. Why are you picking on me anyway?' My voice rises.

'After you sent me that letter? Where would the fun have been in that?' He pauses for a moment, as if deliberating on whether to say anything further or not. He makes the wrong decision. 'We all knew what he was, Dora. Everyone knew, but you. You're so blinkered and sad you probably thought you had something special with him. You probably thought you'd finally found love…' tears fill my eyes, he sees and his hand comes to his mouth, 'Oh my God, you did, didn't you? You thought you'd found love.' He breaks off at this point, not to give me any respite but to laugh. No one joins in and his laughter dies on his lips. 'So much for the sleuthing ability you're apparently famous for. Ned pulled the wool right over your eyes. He had you and all his other women on a rota and you were what he spent his Thursday afternoons doing. You're not the only one who watches, Dora.' And with that, as far as he's concerned, this is over, because he turns away.

Far from it.

'You're not perfect either, Amos. You don't behave as well as you pretend you do. This lot,' and I wave my arms wildly round at the crowd, 'think they know all about you, but they don't.' He turns back to face me. 'I've seen you sneaking around. Creeping in and out of houses where you have no right to be. It's disgusting.'

'I think you should stop there, Dora,' Sally says, her hand on my arm as she tries to get me to sit again. I pull my arm out of her grip.

'No. Everyone should hear what he's been up to.' Amos raises his hand, palm first, towards me.

'Don't.'

'What a surprise. You don't agree that everyone should hear what the high and mighty Amos Chamberlain gets up to when he thinks no one's looking?'

'I'm warning you, Dora. You are completely wrong about this.'

'Let's see, shall we? I've seen you. Popping in on Agnes Peach for cosy mornings. Spending hours with Manda Babcock and even whiling the time away with Jeremy and Petula Cross. And we all know what goes on at their place. Depraved. That's what you are, Amos. You're a dirty old man preying on those in our society who are struggl—.'

'Enough!' His voice comes out as a bellow. It still doesn't stop me. Energy surges through my limbs as I lean into the argument.

'Trying to shut me up won't work. I see you and now everyone else will see you for what you are, too.' He shakes his head.

'You're deluded and have no idea what you're talking about.'

'I've seen you. Don't deny it.'

'I should be flattered you still think I have it in me. But I'm not. I'm appalled and embarrassed for you.'

'Why should I be embarrassed? I'm only telling the truth.'

'No, you're not. What you're spreading is information about people which should be private.' There's a deathly hush in the room. Every eye fixed on the drama.

'Oh yes, I bet you'd like your life to be kept private, wouldn't you? But you've made mine a source of public entertainment tonight. I'm simply reciprocating.'

'Don't hold back on my behalf, Amos,' Jeremy calls from the stage.

Amos nods. 'What you've seen is me being a friend to patients in need. It's a role the surgery has given me under its auspices.' He sways before me, the floor no longer steady beneath my feet.

'What?' This word is barely above a whisper as my stomach drops. The alcohol that swirls there threatens to come back up. He sighs, resigned to having to continue.

'I get asked by the doctor to check in and spend time with patients who, for whatever reason, are housebound.' He flicks his hand towards Jeremy. 'We've been playing chess since his accident.'

'Chess,' I repeat. I'm aware of shuffles around the room now, someone clearing their throat. Embarrassed for me. Heat rises from my chest at my mistake. My face burns, suffused with shame and humiliation.

'Once,' I say, 'just once… that's all I wanted,' and unable to bear all the eyes upon me any longer, I dash for the exit. Slamming the door back against its stopper, I cross the lobby, heave open the main door, the icy wind not slowing my progress as I rush towards home. I hear the door close behind me. Then again. Someone is following. I speed up. Desperate not to be caught.

'Wait up,' I hear shouted, but I don't. I have to get home. I have to get proof of his treachery, because it's finally come to me. After all these years during which I've wanted, waited for him to trip up, to get caught out and for everyone to see him in his true colours, now, right now, right at this exact moment, I've realised I've had the proof all along.

I'm at my front door and scrabble for the key in my pockets, but I don't have it. My bag is back in the hall and I cry out in frustration. Tears fall, my nose snotty, and I wipe it on my sleeve.

'I've got it, Dora. I've got your bag, your key.' Sally is there, and Alice. She scrabbles in my bag, keen to solve my problem, and the moment my key appears, I snatch it from her and scratch around the lock in my haste to get the door open. I dash inside and make for the stairs, kicking off my shoes. I don't turn on the light in my room but strip off my clothes.

'Are you alright?' Alice calls up the stairs. I'm glad they haven't followed me up here. The spies. Sent to watch what I'm up to. Probably by him. They'll lie to my face they're my friends, but I can't trust anyone. They're all on his side. Everyone always has been.

'I'm fine. I'll be down in a minute.' I'm surprised by how normal I sound when my life is imploding.

I dress, check my face in the mirror. It's a mess of smeared makeup, swollen red eyes and nose. I wet some toilet roll, attempt to fix the worst of it. My hands shake, the clean-up ineffectual. I don't want to waste a second, so abandon my efforts and dash back downstairs.

'What the f—' Sally's expletive is interrupted by Alice's, 'Jesus! What's going on?'

181

I take no notice of either as I head for the front door and launch back out into the night. A move they clearly weren't expecting. I have nearly reached the end of the row of cottages before I hear them behind me.

The last time I wore this dress, the points of my shoes peeked out from below the hem. Now, barefoot, I have to lift the skirt until it's clear of the ground as I stride out towards the village hall. The back hem drags on the rough, wet pavement behind. Sally and Alice catch up as I open the main door to the hall. I hear the noise inside which has picked up since I was last there only moments ago.

'Stop!' Alice says. I sense desperation in her voice, but don't understand why. I look magnificent. I know it. This dress. Worn once. Lovingly made by my mother. Still fits like a glove. Simple, elegant, ivory. The veil, long, ornate, flows down my back. Memories flit into my mind of Beth fussing with the folds. Beth. Another lifetime.

Those who witness my return fall silent.

What an entrance.

Take your seats, everyone.

Act 2 is about to begin.

I seek Amos in the crowd. He's at the back of the hall, facing away, still talking to someone out of sight, but turns, no doubt wondering at the silence. I enjoy the look on his face as the blood drains from it. Ashen. He closes the gap between us quickly, reaches to take my elbow as though about to eject me from the room, but I snatch it away.

'What are you doing?' His voice is low, the words said with a snarl.

'What does it look like? Letting your adoring public know exactly what sort of man you are.'

182

'No one will care. Not after all this time. Look at you,' and he actually leans back and looks me up and down. A sneer on his lips. 'You're a drunken mess.'

I spin away from him and walk further down the room to address the audience. 'You may wonder why I have come back dressed like this. Well, it's time you all knew exactly what sort of man the saintly Amos Chamberlain is.' I turn back to look at him, but he is walking away, climbing the steps to the stage to join his cast. 'Turn around and face me, you coward.'

He does so, reluctance etched into every movement. 'Just over fifty years ago, ladies and gentlemen, this man,' and I gesticulate towards Amos, 'Allowed me to go through with the charade of putting this dress on and preparing for our wedding. He had told me he loved me. His last words to me were, "I'll see you in church." Then he let me parade myself in front of all my family and friends, all the village, to walk to a church when he knew he'd no intention of turning up.' I hear gasps around the room. Someone yells 'Shame' from the back and it spurs me on.

'Like an idiot, I waited, thinking something had held him up. I panicked, knowing he must have been in an accident and have been injured not to be there. Because I trusted him.' I pause for effect. To make sure everyone takes in every last syllable. 'I went to the flat that was to be our first home and there our landlady, a woman I'd never even met before, gave me a letter from you.' I make sure I am talking directly to him at this point. He shakes his head and a woman close by tuts. 'You didn't even have the courtesy or courage to tell me in person.'

'Stop it. You're making a fool of yourself,' he says, and makes an action with his hands as though to brush me away. An action which ignites the fury in me once more and as he turns,

183

my control slips, the urge to attack overwhelming. I reach out to grab a glass and hurl it with all my might towards his retreating back. The audience cries out as it hits the back of his head before ricocheting and smashing as it crashes to the floor. He barely flinches, but his hand comes to his head as he turns around. Surprise is written wide on his face. He glances at his hand.

No blood.

He smiles.

Big mistake.

I pick up another glass from the table and this time grunt as I throw it. He ducks and as the other cast members dash for cover, it smashes on the stage behind him. Susannah is by my side, but I won't be held, or controlled, or managed any longer. My frustration erupts as the anger and bitterness at staying quiet for so long can no longer be contained, and I scream as another glass hurtles through the air. Hands reach to grab me, but oblivious to those around me now I slip through them. Determination drives me forward as I leap for the stage. I take the steps two at a time and close in on him. Fear shows in his eyes for the first time.

'Then tonight you had to show me up again in front of everyone.'

'You've done a good enough job without my help.' I ignore his latest put down.

'You must have found my humiliation hilarious. But even I didn't think you'd be so cruel as to add in a baby. Yet you stooped that low. How could you?' My voice is rising, and I'm unable to stop what is coming out of my mouth.

'A baby? You mean Flora's? Why shouldn't I? It's a story. It's made up.'

'Made up? That's what you think of her.'

'Her? You're making no sense.'

'I was pregnant, Amos. Fifty years ago. When you left me. I was pregnant. I had your baby. Now our daughter is out there somewhere in the world without us.' Total silence. There's a moment. A nanosecond. The world nothing but him and me. Face to face. Eye to eye. When I think he gets it. He understands. He believes. He stares at me as though trying to fathom what I said, but it's too little too late, and with a wave of his hand, he breaks the spell holding us and shuts me down.

'You're talking nonsense. There was no baby. And you're drunk. Go home and sleep it off, Dora.' He turns as he dismisses me.

'Don't you dare deny her and don't you walk away from me.' Stopping him is the only thing I focus on as I lunge across the glass-strewn stage. Savage shards slice through skin. Blood spurts. Feet slip. My hands grab his jacket. He spins, brings his arm round with such force it breaks my hold. His other hand follows, bunched as a fist. Pain spears through my jaw as it connects. My head flies back. Feet lift as momentum hurls me from the stage and I crash to the floor below.

People gather as I gasp for air. Faces above peer down at the freak show. Shock reverberates through my body. My head spins, throbs, and I go to touch it. When I look, there is blood on my hand. My fingers wet, tacky. And I stare, shocked at the sight. At the damage I have inflicted.

They'll all blame me for this. Blame me for attacking him. I have to run. Escape. That's what I have to do. I have to get away. Get home before the police get here and I'm locked up for attacking this pillar of the community, Amos.

I try to move. My arm hurts. My feet slip, bloody and wet, as I scrabble to get to my knees. Someone stops me. Forceful hands halt my progress. His people are all around me now; they hold me down and I know this is it. There is no escape. They have got me.

Faces surround and loom in on me. Distorted. Unfocused. Cloaked with disappointment. Heads shake, and I turn my face away with shame.

Sally is close. She says words I can't make head nor tail of. Strokes my hair like she cares, but she's in on it. She's one of them and can't be trusted.

Sirens draw close. Blue lights swirl outside. They come. The police. My imprisoners. Once they take me, they will find out all my crimes. She who abandoned her baby. She who attacks saints. She who has done so much more.

Sally's face grows faint. A uniform in her place. A light is shone in my eyes. Lips move, but I hear no words above the cacophony in my head. I have to get away, but know it's too late, much too late. I struggle but can't speak. My breaths rasp as I gasp for air. They place a board in behind me and I'm strapped to it. Strapped. I fight the restraints as they tighten around my limbs, my head, and I'm rigid with fear. My eyes flit from blur to blur. Mouths open, wide and hollow, imagined venomous words spouted to poison those around. All hope flees as I'm imprisoned against my will. Helpless, I scream... scream. Strain to get away. Scream and fight... It's all I have left. Against my will my body relaxes. Overwhelmed. Drugged. Toxin flows through my veins. Dulls my senses. Until I can't fight anymore. All feeling is gone.

I'm lifted and close my eyes against all those who call themselves my friends yet stand by and do nothing when I'm taken forcibly by those who will do me harm. A blast of cold air hits me as I'm wheeled from the hall and into the bright lights of the ambulance. I recognise no one around me, but know now they have me, I will die. That's why they're here, these kidnappers, these murderers. I wonder what they'll do to me before they kill me, because only one thought consumes me now. Death. They will kill me because of what I've done, and I will never see Rosie again.

23: The Morning After the Night Before

It is 49 years, 364 days since I last saw Rosie.

Chunks of memory are missing from the night. But I am feeling better this morning. Calmer. Drug-induced, no doubt. The restraints are gone. My arm is in plaster, there are stitches in my head and my jaw is tender, bruised and uncomfortable to move. My bandaged feet stick up like icebergs under the snowy sheet. I remember none of this treatment taking place.

Every part of me aches.

With difficulty I turn on my side in the hospital bed, bringing my knees up to make myself small.

The doctors have done their rounds. They stood around my bed, doctors and students, and talked of my psychosis as if I was not there. I did not know what they meant and was too intimidated to ask. But I am told a psychiatrist is coming to see me later. Perhaps they will tell me when I can go home.

While I wait, I struggle to piece together the previous evening. My thoughts are muddled with an inability to differentiate fact from fiction. Truth from lie. Flashes of memory bring heat to my cheeks. The faces of horrified onlookers vivid in a way they had not been last night. The shame. What will everyone think of me? Of my behaviour? It was all so mortifyingly public. I can never go out again. The thought of ever facing my friends, should they even still be my friends, is one embarrassment too far.

A student earlier asked why this had happened to me. I strained for the answer, but there was nothing definite forthcoming as the group moved on up the ward.

The question has stayed with me all day. Why? Why me? Why now?

24: The Trigger Point?

Five years ago.

The day I killed Evelyn remains etched in my mind.

I did not set out with that intention. To kill her. In fact, despite her living the life I should have had, I had never felt much animosity towards her, only irritation. Because she could be incredibly annoying. But one day, means, motive and opportunity coincided and I snapped. It is the only explanation I can give. Fortunately, I have never had to because no one has ever suspected me. Why would they? It was an accident.

At least that is what everyone believes.

Some may think I killed her because I wanted Amos for myself, but that could not be further from the truth. I mean, obviously once I had wanted him, otherwise I would never have agreed to marry him, but I certainly don't want him now. Not with the state he is in at his time of life. All the vitality sucked out of him by the stresses and strains of living a life packed full of work and family commitments. All that ear hair. No thank you.

I might not have planned it, but it was actually ridiculously easy to kill Evelyn. Who knew life hung by so fragile a thread?

I had had a terrible day. I was coming down with a cold. An everyday hazard when working around children, you are always fighting something off. Anyway, I was due to retire shortly and had wanted to glide through the last few months with little trouble. Instead, we had had a new computer system installed, which I was meant to embed but nothing was running smoothly.

I couldn't print off the registers, access the pupil records or update the finances needed for meetings the next day. The Head was constantly on at me and all I wanted was to go back to the days when we worked on paper and never had this sort of tension in the office. Because of the problems and the IT people being unable to sort out the issues until the afternoon, I had to work late, and being midwinter it had been dark for hours by the time I left school. It had not got above freezing all day, an easterly wind bringing sub-zero temperatures with it, and I had had to de-ice and scrape down the windscreen for the second time. I shivered as I got behind the wheel, knowing the car would barely get warm before I got home.

At least I did not have to stop off anywhere on the way. I had had the foresight to pop into Sharon's Stores that morning for a few bits and pieces, knowing it was cold enough to stay fresh in the car for the day.

I could not wait to get in, get the fire going, slip into something more comfortable and warmer, and eat a satisfying dinner. Parking several doors down from my cottage, I was annoyed all over again because by being late, I had missed out on my usual parking space. Yet another irritation to add to the most aggravating day I had had in a while. I got out of the car and opened the boot to get my shopping out.

'You alright, Dora,' made me jump, and I banged my head on the underside of the boot because I hadn't yet opened it fully. I winced and brought one hand up to rub my head.

'Sorry. Didn't mean to make you jump.' There was a giggle, as though she thought it funny. I wrapped one hand through the plastic shopping bag handles and looked out from under the boot lid. It was dark, the nearest streetlamp a hundred metres away.

'Hello, Evelyn.'

'You're late home tonight.'

'Yes, I got held up.'

'What a pity you're not already retired like me. Amos wouldn't hear of me carrying on after he'd stopped, which was lovely of him, don't you think?'

'Lovely, yes.'

'Isn't it a shame you've got no one waiting at home for you? Look at your cottage, all shrouded in darkness. You should get some of those timer switches, set them so some lamps come on and make it a bit more welcoming.'

'Yes. Yes, I should do that.' I was exhausted and could do without one of her advice sessions.

'I've left my man well fed and happy and I'm off to the bingo at the village hall.'

I had planned to go, purely because it is what I do, but after the day I'd had could not think of anything worse.

'Watch your footing. It's icy tonight.'

'Oh, you sound just like Amos. He's always going on at me the same. You'd have made a great pair. Shame I nabbed him off you, eh.' And she giggled again as she turned away.

And that was it.

The final straw.

She was only a few metres away as I launched myself in her direction; I swung my shopping bag up to around shoulder height and spun it towards her like I was a shot-putter that had forgotten to let go. I was not sure what I expected to gain by this action. The few items in my bag were more likely to be damaged by her than she by them. As if she sensed me coming, she turned, but it was too late. As the contents of my bag collided with the back of her head, her feet shot out from under her. She

192

crashed to the icy pavement with little more than a grunt as the air whooshed out of her. I inhaled sharply at what I had done. My hand to my mouth, wondering how I was going to explain hitting her, I fumbled for the apology I needed to make as soon as she got up.

But there was no movement.

I knelt beside her. Stockinged knees soaked through, ice cold against the hard pavement. I peered at her face. Her eyelids flickered.

'Evelyn,' I said, as I shook her shoulder. She moaned.

She could hear me.

This woman who gloated about nabbing my husband.

This woman who thought she knew best.

This woman who believed she knew everything.

It irked me she didn't.

Not the most important thing.

This woman who rubbed it in my face about what a great pair we would have made.

I agreed. We would have.

She was still, no improvement in her consciousness, and I should get help. I should. I knew I should. But first I took the opportunity.

I leaned over. My face above hers.

'Amos and I had a child, Evelyn. Her name is Rosie. We made her from love.'

The release of those words said out loud surged through me like an adrenaline rush. I sat back on my heels, glanced up the empty street, and blew out my held breath. When I looked back, her eyes were open.

She stared as though she could see into my soul.

Fear jolted through me.

She had heard.

And now she would tell.

She wasn't making any attempt at further movement, but she would, given time.

My only thought, to stop her.

I leaned across her once more, took hold of a bunch of hair at each side of her head. Expelling a grunt with the effort, I lifted her head from the pavement until her shoulders rose. A dead weight. I slammed it back onto the tarmac. The wet splat it made as it landed turned my stomach.

There was blood on my hand. My fingers wet, tacky. And I stared, shocked at the sight. At the damage I had inflicted.

My murderous hands shook in my lap as I looked into her face.

There was no movement.

None. At. All.

I needed to check, and shook her gently. Called her name. Nothing.

What had I done?

Fear drained the strength from my limbs. Maybe it wasn't too late? Maybe she would be all right? If I got her some help. Yes, that was it. Evelyn needed my help, and I struggled to my feet, as the cold had seized my stiffened joints. Glancing around again, I could see there was still no one about on this bitter night. I was going to have to get Amos. I moved my bag back to near the car and hurried across the road, hammered on the door. It opened, as I was about to pound on it again, fist lifted. A frown on his face. 'What do you want?'

'It's Evelyn,' and I pointed across the road to the dark mass on the ground.

'What?' He craned his neck. 'What's happened to her?' He pushed me to one side as he took a couple of steps down the path.

'I just got home from work and there she was,' truth and lie tumbled out together in the rush of words, 'she's not moving.'

'Call an ambulance.' He pointed to his front door, turned and rushed towards his wife.

I took my first ever step into their home. The phone was on a small round table in the hall. I dialled 999. There were few questions I could answer, but once assured the emergency services were on the way, I hung up. Unable to resist the opportunity, I took a step towards the door I knew would lead to the sitting room and pushed it open. I got little more than a feeling of warmth and comfort from the colours and furnishings before the guilt at being there made me uncomfortable. But, seeing a wool throw on the arm of the sofa, I reached for it as my excuse for my nosey in and scuttled out of the cottage as quickly as possible.

I rushed across the road, my breath frozen clouds in the air.

'Is she breathing?'

'Yes,' was Amos's curt response. He had put her in the recovery position. I covered her with the throw. He looked up and gave me a grateful smile.

'It is freezing,' I said, by way of explanation. 'The ambulance is on its way.'

'She must have slipped on the ice. I told her to be careful.' He sounded annoyed, and I was not sure if it was at her for being careless or at his inability to protect her. 'She'd only just left our house. Didn't you see what happened?'

'No, I must have pulled up shortly after.' I was already wondering if I could see this through. This lie. What if the injuries did not tally with my story? Surely it would be better to admit what happened now and get it over with? But how would I explain me purposely bashing her head against the ground? The rush of blood with the initial swing of my shopping bag was one thing. But that, entirely another.

And what if she was seriously hurt, and everyone found out I attacked her? She was so popular in the village. Everyone would hate me. No, I could not say anything. I could not let the truth come out. It was too late anyway, I convinced myself. The moment when I should have told the truth to Amos had already slipped past.

'I will get another cover for her.'

'Thank you.' But he did not look up from where he knelt at the side of his unconscious wife.

I picked up the bag of shopping and hurried to my cottage. I fished out the keys and, as my hands still shook, had difficulty getting the right one into the lock in my rush.

As thoughts swirled in my mind like snowflakes in a storm, I struggled to get them straight to work out what happened. Maybe I was not the cause of this accident. Surely, me hitting her would have pushed her forward, not backward, therefore she must have lost her footing at the same time. Perhaps it was destiny for her to fall and hit her head?

Perhaps it was. And if I had gone for help immediately, it was one thing. But I had not. And there was no escaping that.

I had put the bag of shopping on the worktop. There was a solid clunk as it landed. I was not sure what I had bought that would have made such a noise, so I opened the bag. There was a sticky packet of biscuits, now crumbs inside the plastic. A half dozen eggs, smashed. Damp patches had soaked through the box, and there was egg goo over everything. A chicken, on offer. Bought fresh this morning. Now frozen solid. A lethal weapon.

Shaking, I left the kitchen, rushed upstairs to the airing cupboard and pulled out a couple of blankets. I collected a torch on my way back to the street and found Amos had not moved. He was stroking her hair. I opened up the blankets and covered Evelyn up better, tucking them in around her inert body. I flicked on the torch and wished I hadn't. It revealed what Amos had not seen before, what he had not known about. The blood. Enough to wet the pavement. The back of her head matted.

'Oh my God,' he groaned, his hands coming up to his head. Nauseous, for a moment I thought I was going to vomit. But blue lights could be seen spinning in the distance and thus distracted I took a couple of deep breaths.

'Thank goodness.' I stood back now help had arrived. Not that I had done much, anyway. The paramedics were soon at Evelyn's side, although they had some difficulty moving Amos at first. He was still on his knees and I put my hands on his shoulders, encouraged him to give them space so they could do their work. He did, reluctantly though, so concerned was he with Evelyn. I don't think he even knew I was there.

The ambulance drew attention to the drama unfolding in the street. Curtains pulled back, front doors opened, as neighbours peered out to see what was going on. Alice Fraser approached and asked if there was anything she could do. A couple from over the road appeared. Him with a large coat for Amos. Her with a flask of coffee which she offered to everyone present.

As the paramedics checked Evelyn over, I got another shock when a police car pulled up and an officer got out. He checked in with the paramedics who told him, and us, Evelyn was stable but still unconscious, so they would be taking her to hospital. He moved closer to us.

'Mr Chamberlain?' Amos nodded, not taking his eyes from Evelyn as they lifted her onto a stretcher. The police officer turned his attention to me. 'And you are?'

'Dora Smith. I'm a neighbour,' and I gesticulated over my shoulder towards my cottage. 'I found Evelyn, told Amos, and called for an ambulance. Why are you here?'

'I was in the area and was sent to check on what happened to Mrs Chamberlain. Did you witness the fall?' Amos said nothing, wanting to move away and follow Evelyn.

'No, and I doubt anyone did. They would surely have stayed with her if they had. I found her when I got home from work and there wasn't anyone else around then. She must have slipped on the ice and hit her head.' I prayed he did not want to question me further. That he did not want to come back to my cottage where the weapon used to fell Evelyn was lying on my kitchen worktop.

The paramedics told Amos they were about to leave. I heard him ask if he could travel with her, but they were not keen and asked if he had a car. When he said he did, they suggested he drive to the hospital separately.

He now walked away from me and the police officer, who called after him, 'Mr Chamberlain, I need to ask you some questions.'

'You'll have to come to the hospital then. I have to be there when Evelyn wakes up,' he said, and carried on walking. We both watched in silence as he went back into his cottage and came out again almost immediately with his car keys. Moments later, he had driven off, and we were alone.

I bent to retrieve the blankets and throw the paramedics had left on the pavement and turned back to the police officer. 'Have you finished with me? Only I could do with getting inside. I am freezing.'

'I have some questions. Could I come in now to ask them?'

'Would it be alright if we did it tomorrow? I am exhausted and obviously shaken.' He assessed me briefly.

'Okay. I'll come back in the morning.' This reassured me. He could not think I had committed a crime, or he would have wanted to come in immediately to ask his questions, or maybe even take me to the station. As it was, he saw an older lady who was out after dark and was cold and tired. Which was exactly what I wanted him to see.

Utterly drained as I re-entered my home, I dropped the bundle I was carrying on the floor of the small hall and closed the front door. I made my way to the kitchen and surveyed the mess. Egg had seeped out of the bag, puddled on the worktop, and was now dripping onto the floor. I fished into the bag and retrieved the chicken, no softer than it was the last time I touched it. Turning on the tap, I washed the outer cellophane, now tacky with egg, then placed it on the surface.

I lit the oven, unwrapped the chicken, putting it in a baking tin, before covering it with foil. I brought the bin close to the worktop, then scooped the bag and the rest of the ruined shopping into it, cleaning down the worktop and floor after. The oven was now up to temperature, and I put the chicken inside. It wasn't ideal to cook it from frozen but it was the best I could do.

I had considered throwing the chicken away too, but what if the police inspected my rubbish? It would look odd, wouldn't it, to have thrown away a perfectly good chicken? The rest of it,

199

fair enough, I could explain I had dropped the bag with the shock of finding Evelyn and the items were beyond use. Quite what I was going to do with the chicken once cooked, I didn't know. I was certain it would choke me if I ate any, but I would think about that tomorrow.

I pondered how things were going at the hospital. If Evelyn was awake yet. If, even now, she was telling everyone what I had done to her. If she was telling Amos about Rosie. As a result, my nerves were shredded. I could not eat despite only a short time ago my stomach rumbling as I drove home from work. I made up the fire but could not get warm, the chill having made its way right into my bones.

I opened a bottle of wine, needing the alcohol to take the edge off my nerves.

Why did I tell her? I had held on to my secret for so long, why spill it now? I could not fathom my behaviour but had to admit it had possibly been driven purely by the desire for her to know. Her cruel words about nabbing Amos goaded me, of course. Following on from years of similar taunts from her. Plus, there had been the opportunity to have the last word. Which I didn't think had ever happened before.

The last word.

What if I had killed her and it really was?

I put the television on for some distraction, but could not focus on anything. A couple of hours later, the smell of the chicken roasting, usually so comforting, permeated through from the kitchen and sickened me. I went through to check it. Made sure it was cooked right through and left it to cool on the top.

From habit I got ready for bed but doubted I would sleep, my mind whirling with the events of the evening and filled with worries about what was happening at the hospital. Were the police present? When Evelyn woke and told them what happened, would they charge me with assault? Were they right at this moment about to knock on my door to arrest me? I could not bear the kerfuffle it would cause. Imagine the gossip. The humiliation. And, worst of all, the speculation about why I did what I did. I could see it all coming out and there being little sympathy for me. The vengeful ex. Hardly. It had been years. Could anyone realistically still be vengeful after that length of time?

Once ready for bed, I returned to the kitchen and put the chicken in the fridge. I would decide what to do with it in the morning.

I heard a sound outside, a door slamming, and I returned to the bay window to look out again. I could see nothing, but it had been the same all evening. At the slightest noise, I had jumped up to peer out into the street, hoping it would be Amos, with good news. On this occasion, I would have gone out to intercept him, to find out what had happened.

Hoping it would not be the police, about to arrest me.

I had a headache coming. A tension behind my eyes with the strain of the evening, and I drank some water and went to bed. But I still could not settle. I read and although the pages turned, the words did not go in. I switched off the light, lay in the dark and, against my better nature, said a prayer for Evelyn. It had been years since I had prayed, despite being a regular attendee at the church. Although of course, I was only that because of their involvement. Amos was a bell ringer. Evelyn was on the flower rota, like me, but where she had a natural flair for the activity, I did not.

In the early hours, I fell into an exhausted, restless sleep, my dreams vivid and violent. I woke with a start shortly after six. I got up to look out of the window. No sign of Amos' car. I imagined him on one of those hard plastic chairs at Evelyn's bedside and possibly alone.

Their daughters, Cheryl and Amelia, might have been called, of course. Mind you, they both lived at some distance and had other commitments. High-powered jobs, families. Who knew how quickly they would be able to get there?

I considered the idea of going into the hospital later to visit. Amos, usually, would not welcome such an intrusion. I knew him only too well. But surely this was different. Having found her I had an interest in finding out how Evelyn was.

My headache was worse, so I took a couple of pills and got ready for the day. A shower would make me feel better and some food, I thought. My stomach was more settled than the previous evening and I was hungry.

Once dressed, I made my way downstairs and had to step around the pile I had left there the previous evening. The throw I took through to the kitchen and popped into the washing machine. The blankets I folded into a neat pile and put on the work surface above. They were wet in places and dirty along the edges but fortunately there was no blood, as far as I could see, but as they were wool, I would clean them later.

I filled the washing machine with enough to make a load and put it on.

I took the milk out of the fridge for my tea and spotted the chicken. Guilt washed over me in a wave once more as nausea flooded my stomach. I still persevered with making some breakfast and took it through to the front room as always to eat it at my table in the window. I kept the light off so no one would spot me sitting there.

It was Saturday morning and there was little activity outside, although gradually the village came to life. The milkman, Harry with the newspapers, the postman, did their rounds. The only distraction from them came when a letter dropped onto my mat. I held my breath as always and crossed my fingers as I bent to pick it up. Maybe this was the day when I would hear from her. Maybe this was the day when she reached out. I knew I was about to be disappointed before I even turned it over. The envelope was too big to be a personal letter. Too corporate. Sure enough, it was from my electricity suppliers, and the bubble of hope that had briefly risen descended again into the pit of my stomach.

I refreshed the pot of tea and took my place in the window again. Neighbours passed: walking dogs, going to the shop, chatting with each other. A couple pointed to the spot where Evelyn fell last night. The rumour mill grinding into action. I wondered when the police officer would be back.

Amos returned shortly before ten. I did not know what this meant. Was it good he was back home, as it showed Evelyn was on the mend? Or bad that he had returned rather than being with her in the hospital? He reversed his car into its spot and took a deep breath before reaching for his keys and getting out. I adjusted myself in my chair, leaning forward slightly in anticipation of what came next. I was eager to know of Evelyn's progress, but didn't know how he would react if I went over for an update.

To my surprise, rather than turn to his home, he faced mine and crossed the road.

I rose from my seat, although allowed a few seconds to pass after he knocked on the door for me to open it. I could not remember him ever coming to my door before.

He was grey with exhaustion.

'Amos, how is she?'

'Evelyn died a couple of hours ago.' I gasped. My breath caught in my throat, my hand on my chest.

'Oh no. I am sorry.' He nodded and looked down. 'I can't believe it. She only fell. How could that have killed her? Sorry,' I added quickly, realising the brutality of my words.

'It's alright. They're not sure what happened, so a post-mortem will be done.'

'Of course. Yes, it makes sense. Is there anything I can do?' He shook his head.

'You've done enough already.' He cleared his throat and for one moment I thought he knew and was about to lay into me with his accusations, so there was enormous relief when he continued, 'Thank you for looking after her.' Guilt rose in me like a buoy on the high tide and there was a moment, the briefest moment, when I almost blurted out what I had done. But I didn't. I held it in, tamped it down along with my other secret, afraid of the trouble I would be in should the truth come out.

He turned away abruptly. As he crossed the road, another car pulled up. Inside were both his daughters. I closed the door softly and hung my head.

A post-mortem would be done.

Evelyn's death had swept away one set of worries for me. Although guilty relief was my overwhelming emotion that she could no longer tell anyone what she knew. But another set had come to the fore. What if the post-mortem revealed there was

204

more than one blow to the back of her head? Could it show that? I had no idea.

And how long would it take for it to be done, and the truth revealed?

Again, I did not have a clue.

I needed to keep busy, and went through to the kitchen. There was one thing I could do, and that was to get rid of the chicken. I heated a pan on the stovetop, added oil and chopped an onion which I fried off along with some bacon and a sliced-up leek. I stripped the flesh from the bones of the chicken. Queasy. My stomach turned as I did so. I added flour to the pan, some stock and a few other vegetables, carrots, sweetcorn and peas. Finally, I added in the chicken and left it to cook on a low heat.

I washed up, and it was as I was taking off my rubber gloves that I heard the knock on the door. The police. It must be. I did not bother checking out of the window first as I would usually do, but simply opened the door. Daylight showed him to be much younger than I had thought last night.

'Mrs Smith?'

'Miss,' I corrected. 'Although please call me Dora.' Best to be friendly.

'Dora.' He gave the briefest of smiles. 'I'm sorry, but I've come with bad news.'

'About Evelyn? Amos has already told me. It's such a sad thing to have happened.' A crease formed between his eyebrows.

'Oh, he came over? I understood you were not on the best of terms.'

'I would not put it like that. We rub along easily enough. We are just not friends. People keep to themselves around here, anyway. But I suppose because I was the one who found her, he

205

came to tell me when he got back a short while ago.' I stopped, realising I was talking too much.

'I see; do you think I could come in? I have some questions to ask.'

'Of course. Sorry, where are my manners? It is bitterly cold still,' and I stood back to open the door wide and ushered him into the sitting room. I followed him in to go through to the kitchen. 'Would you like a cup of tea or coffee?'

'I'd appreciate a coffee, please. Thank you. White, no sugar.' I made one for us both and carried them back through to the sitting room. He took a seat at one end of the sofa, me at the other. I could see him looking around, taking everything in. He took out a notepad, laid it on his knee, and retrieved a pencil from his pocket.

'Do you live here alone?'

'Yes.'

'And you work locally?'

'Yes, at the primary school in the next village. I am the school secretary.' He nodded, although I was not sure what that had to do with anything.

'And I gather you were late home last night?'

'Yes. I'd had a terrible day. One of those where everything goes wrong. We had some IT issues and the technician could not get there to sort out the problem until late in the day.'

'And do you usually park on the road there?'

'No. If I get home on time, I park in front of my house. But I guess fate played its part last night, because if I hadn't parked where I did, I may well not have seen her.

'Indeed. Talk me through what happened.'

'I pulled up. Got out and went to get my shopping from the boot. I stepped up over the verge and onto the pavement and that's when I saw her.'

'Not until then?'

'No, she was further down from where I had parked and right in the dark spot between the street lights.' I felt my heartbeat rise as he questioned my actions.

'What did you do next?'

'I dropped my shopping and went to see who it was.'

'You couldn't tell already?'

'No, it wasn't until I was right over her.'

'Was she conscious?'

'No, I called her name, shook her shoulder gently, but there was no response. Then I went over to get Amos.'

He looked at his notepad on which he had been scribbling as we talked. 'According to the times I have down here, Mrs Chamberlain could only have just fallen over. She'd not long left the house.' I nodded. 'Did you see anyone else around?'

'No, there was no one. It was a bitterly cold evening, as you know. People round here tend to get indoors and batten down the hatches in weather like this. Only a few came out even after the ambulance arrived.' I hesitated, then had to ask. 'Do you suspect foul play?' I second-guessed the words as soon as they were out of my mouth. Was that a phrase anyone used nowadays?

'Probably not. But when someone is found in unexplained circumstances, we're duty bound to ask a few questions. Make sure nothing untoward has happened.'

'And you think something untoward may have happened here?'

'Not necessarily. But it's unusual for someone to die from a fall such as this.' Which was exactly what I had said to Amos earlier. I remembered the blood, the wet on the pavement, and gasped. He looked at me with concern. 'What is it?'

'Sorry, I just remembered the blood. It was on the pavement. Should I take something out there to clear it away? I wouldn't want Amos or one of the girls to see it.'

'Don't worry. Someone else has already dealt with it.' I was relieved. It wasn't a job I would have wanted. He looked at his notepad and I thought back to his words.

Nothing untoward.

My thoughts wandered for a moment. Maybe she would have fallen anyway, even if I had not hit her. His next question brought me back into the here and now.

'Why do you think Evelyn was out at that time of night?'

'Oh, she was off to the bingo,' I answered, far too quickly.

'How do you know?' His brow furrowed as the acid in my stomach curdled its contents at my mistake.

'She told me, earlier in the week, when we were at book group.' She had done no such thing. Amos and Evelyn never shared where they were going with me for fear I would be there too, and I hoped he was not already aware of that. 'I was planning on going, but having worked late had already decided on the way home to give it a miss.' My heart fluttered like it had wings, my breaths shallow.

'It's a surprise there was no one else out and about who was also going to the bingo.'

'True.' I had not considered that. 'Although Evelyn was one of those people who is,' and I paused to correct myself, 'sorry, was always late everywhere. She might have just been unlucky that anyone coming from this direction had already passed.'

'I see.' He closed his notepad, and realising this was nearly over I relaxed. 'I didn't see any shopping when I arrived last night?' A question which reminded me not to lower my guard.

'No, I had taken it in when I went to get a couple more blankets to keep Evelyn warm.'

'Not too damaged from being dropped, I hope.'

'Oh well, the fall broke the eggs, along with the biscuits, but the chicken survived.' I gesticulated towards the kitchen.

'It smells delicious.'

'Thank you, I think I'll take it over to the Chamberlains later. Their daughters have arrived and I doubt they will want to be cooking.'

'That's a kind gesture.' He looked over at my table in the bay window. The solitary chair. 'I bet you see all sorts from there.' He finished his coffee.

I shrugged. 'Sometimes. But mostly it is day-to-day normal things. Helps me not to feel quite so alone.' He nodded as if he understood, but I could not imagine he had a clue how long a day could be when there was no one to share it with. He stood as if he was about to go. 'Is that it?'

'I think so. I'll be in touch if the post-mortem reveals anything further.' My mouth was dry, and I reached for my coffee and drained the mug before standing beside him. He paused for a moment. Looked out of the window.

'Just one other thing.' He said this as if it had only then occurred to him. 'Have you seen anything from here that I should know about Mr and Mrs Chamberlain?' This took me by surprise. Was Amos a suspect? I had been so wrapped up in my own issues, I had not considered how the situation might appear to an outsider.

I shook my head. 'No, absolutely not. They are such a lovely family. Two girls. Left home now, of course. But they are close. This will devastate them all.' I was pleased with myself that despite the opportunity presented to me I had said nothing to cast suspicion on Amos.

He nodded, hesitating a moment longer as he continued to stare across at the Chamberlains' cottage. Then he snapped out of whatever thought process was going on and looked back at me. 'Thank you for the coffee, and your time. It's much appreciated.'

'You are welcome,' I said, and followed him to the front door and watched as he headed over the road to Amos'. Maybe he had questions for them or possibly he was reporting back on what he had found out over here. I checked from my vantage point to see how much time he spent over there. It was not long. Not as long as he was here. When he exited again through their gate, he gazed over at my window, checking to see if I was watching, but I knew the nets gave me all the privacy I needed.

I ran through the conversation I had had with the police officer. Wondering if I gave anything away I should not have done, and on the whole I was satisfied. Apart from the sticky patch about where Evelyn was going, I did alright.

I checked on the casserole, and it was ready. Although I would usually taste it for seasoning, I couldn't face doing so. The thought alone made me gag. But I added a sprinkle of salt and pepper, just in case and poured it into a large plastic box. I stuck on a label in case they were inundated by the village. Although I had not seen anyone else arrive at their door yet, once word got out, they would be, and the limited space in the freezer would be filled.

I put a thick coat on for the quick journey across the road. The police officer's arrival had shown me the outside world was still well below freezing. I took care crossing and noticed someone had also scattered grit along the pavements on each side. Shame it was too late.

I knocked on Amos' door nervously and was pleased it was Amelia who answered. Her eyes looked sore from crying, and she had a tissue scrunched up in her hand.

'I am sorry for your loss, Amelia.'

'Thank you, Miss Smith.' Her voice was tight with tension, but I noted her use of my formal name. No matter how old she got, and she's five years younger than my Rosie, she would always know me as the school secretary and speak to me accordingly.

'I wanted to drop this over. I doubt you will want to cook.' She smiled as she took the box from my hands.

'Thank you, that's kind of you.' I waved away her thanks.

'It can go in the freezer if you do not want it now.' I was finding it difficult to talk. Emotion threatened to release tears with each word. 'I'll leave you in peace, but you know where I am if I can do anything to help.'

It was not until later that I realised what I had done. As I contemplated this, I also considered my inability to taste the casserole. It was as if a switch had been flicked and the mere thought of meat nauseated me. I knew I would never eat it again.

A few days later, I met Cheryl in the street. She was leaving the shop as I was about to enter.

She paused as I said good morning, which gave me the opportunity to ask how everyone was.

'As well as can be expected,' she said. 'Dad is struggling, as you can imagine.'

'I hope you do not mind my asking, but is there any news on the post-mortem yet?'

'Oh, yes. She died from the blunt trauma to the back of her head from slipping over. Just one of those bizarre things, I think. It caused a haemorrhage, and that was that.' Cheryl had always been the more practical of the two girls. She said all this without shedding a tear, something I doubted Amelia would have managed. 'Oh, and can I thank you for the delicious casserole? We ate it the same day. I'll drop the box back on your doorstep at some point.'

After swallowing to dislodge the lump that had formed in my throat, I said there was no need to rush with it and offered my help again, as one does, and we passed on our way.

I was in the clear, and while the relief was tremendous, my guilt meant I could not celebrate the moment.

I felt bad. Probably always would.

Because there was no getting past the facts.

I had gotten away with murder, and they had eaten the evidence.

25: Mother's Day

It is Mother's Day and for the first time in nearly fifty years I am not at home.

Usually, I would have been anxious I was not there, but whatever they have given me has made me less so. I am resigned. For now. I know I need to ask the next nurse I see for some paper, for I have a letter to write. That is my task for the day. Otherwise, I can do nothing but lie in my hospital bed and think about Rosie. About how she is spending her fiftieth birthday.

Meanwhile, in Melton…

In her cottage…

The phone rings…

The End

Thank you for reading. If you can leave a few words as a review on any retail site of your choice, Goodreads, BookBub or any place of your choosing, then you will feel the warmth of my thanks in the form of a virtual hug. It really does matter as it helps inform other readers whether they should pick up this book or not.

The fourth novel in the *A Shade Darker* series will be released on the 1st April 2025.

Get Free Exclusive Content by Signing up to the Georgia Rose Newsletter

You have got this far, so thank you again for reading *Hard to Forgive*. I really enjoy interacting with my readers and love to build that relationship via my newsletter. If you sign up to that via my website, I will send you **some content that's only available to my subscribers**, for free.

Acknowledgements

As always, a huge thank you is due to my beta (test) readers. This time Claire Millington, Katherine Winters, Kathy Sapsed, Andrew Moore, Debra Cartledge, Clare O'Callaghan and Sarah Postins were exposed to my work at a horribly rough stage as I like early feedback, and I thank them for their candour and for telling me what they really thought (even though I know it's difficult!); it informs my way forward.

I was delighted to work with Mark Barry again as he has always been a fierce champion of my books. He took on the task of editor for *Hard to Forgive* and in never failing to tell me when my words were not good enough has made it considerably better. Thank you.

There are countless punctuation and grammar rules and I consider myself truly blessed, and mightily relieved, to have met Julia Gibbs who knows them all! A great big thank you goes to her for her diligence in proofreading my work so that the final product is as polished as it can be. Any errors that remain are mine and mine alone.

I feel fortunate to have been introduced to the wonderfully patient Simon Emery who has designed this fabulous cover and the map. I thank him for his expertise and I am delighted with the end result.

There are a few who have made a contribution to this novel, whether they realised it or not, and they deserve a special mention. Richard Brown, I thank you for the opening line. You wrote that to me once on an email and I have never forgotten it.

Several years ago the now much missed Gordon Reffin told me of a poster he had seen at his doctors' surgery asking for patient visitors. He thought this would make a story designed to create misunderstandings. But it was one he would never write. So, Gordon, here it is. I only wish I'd finished it earlier.

Thank you to John and Mary Sissons who met me for coffee one day and asked what I was working on. It was while chatting to them about this plot that the psychosis element of the climax revealed itself. Thank you for the inspiration, I hope it worked for you.

And to Andrew Moore, prolific writer of all the murder mystery plots that have taken place in the village I live in, thank you for so generously sharing your creation, *The Poison Pen,* with me. For those who love running or taking part in murder mystery events you may be disappointed that the killer of Ted Fadds was never revealed. But do not fear, for Andrew has agreed for me to distribute copies (together with his catalogue of plots and details of how to get extra ones if you desire) with all proceeds going to a charity of my choice, which will be

Hunts Community Cancer Network. So, if you want to see *The Poison Pen* through to its bitter end do get in touch.

My thanks, as always, goes to the incredibly generous online community of authors, readers, bloggers and reviewers. Much to my surprise, finding all of you has been one of the most enjoyable aspects of becoming an independent author and I thank you for your friendship, knowledge and support.

I thank everyone on my mailing list for signing up to find out more. I love hearing from you and I particularly thank all those who have taken on the challenge of being on my ARC (Advance Reader Copy) team. Your early help (including the error spotting!) and support means a great deal. Let's hope you like what you have just read.

Thank you to all the members of Hunts Writers whose company I enjoy. But a special thank you goes to Sally, Fliss, John and Angie who do all the things I cannot.

Last, but by no means least, is the thank you that goes to my growing family. They have to put up with the actual process of me trying to get a book out and while my grown-up children have now largely escaped most of that, my husband has not. So, Russell, thank you once again for putting up with me through all the times when my thoughts are focused on my fictional world and on getting the work done. x

Contact details

Thank you for reading this far. I'm always interested to hear from readers with any feedback, thoughts or observations they are willing to make. If you'd like to get in touch, or you want to hear about what's coming next, I can be found in all of these places:

My website at Georgia Rose Books where you will also have the opportunity to follow my blog or get some free exclusive content by joining my mailing list.

I'm on X/Twitter @GeorgiaRoseBook

On Facebook or you can 'like' the Georgia Rose – Author page.

I'm easy to find on BookBub and Goodreads too, as well as Instagram and Pinterest (although I have absolutely no idea what I'm meant to be doing on those sites!)

Finally, if you have enjoyed reading this, please tell ~~someone~~ *everyone* you know and, whatever you think of it, if you can, would you consider leaving a review? Of whatever rating! You might not think your opinion matters, but I can assure you it does. It helps the book gain visibility, and it informs other readers whether or not to purchase it, so if you could take a minute or two to leave a few words on the retail site of your choice and/or Goodreads and BookBub that would be hugely appreciated.

Now, you're sitting there holding a beautiful paperback or hardback in your hand and maybe thinking that request doesn't include me... please think again. It doesn't matter how or where you bought your book, all the sites will still accept a review from you.

Thank you.

Printed in Great Britain
by Amazon

38787024R00138